I run up the broad steps to the veranda and put my key in the front-door lock. There is some resistance, and I bend over to look closer. The door is unlocked, and there is a small piece of that invisible cellophane tape over the side, to keep the lock from closing.

I am suddenly alert, with a shivery feeling at the back of my neck. Is someone in our house?

THE KIDNAPPING OF CHRISTINA LATTIMORE

JOAN LOWERY NIXON

HARCOURT, INC.

Orlando   Austin   New York   San Diego   Toronto   London

www.HarcourtBooks.com

First Harcourt paperback edition 2004

The Library of Congress has cataloged the
hardcover edition as follows:
Nixon, Joan Lowery.
The kidnapping of Christina Lattimore/Joan Lowery Nixon.
p. cm.
Summary: A teenage girl is kidnapped, but when freed,
is accused of masterminding the scheme to extort money
from her wealthy grandmother.
[1. Kidnapping—Fiction.
2. Mystery and detective stories.]
I. Title.
PZ7.N65Ki 1979
[Fic] 78-20570
ISBN 0-15-205031-0 pb

Text set in Minister Book
Designed by Scott Piehl

K M O P N L

Printed in the United States of America

To Kathleen Nixon Brush,
with love and appreciation

THE
KIDNAPPING
OF
CHRISTINA
LATTIMORE

[ONE]

I DON'T LIKE the way he's looking at me. It's a kind of creepy look as though the two of us shared some kind of secret, and it's making me uncomfortable.

He's the counterman here at this hamburger place—a tall, stoop-shouldered, skinny guy with dull blond hair that always looks dirty. His beery friends in their sweat-stained shirts, who hunch over the counter talking and laughing in short burps, call him Zack. I don't like the way Zack is staring at me.

He's never done that before, and Lorna and I have been in here countless times. We come in every Friday after class lets out at Madame

DeJon's school for girls. It's our way of celebrating our freedom for another weekend.

I guess it's my idea that we come here. Lorna's a good friend in spite of the fact that she always follows Madame DeJon's rules and looks ready to enter the portals of the River Oaks Country Club at any given moment. She'd be happy to stop for something to eat in Sakowitz's garden tearoom, except that I like to come to this greasy hamburger place, which is really the pits. It's all done in a faded red and white, with the pattern on the floor nearly rubbed out, and it faces the frantic Katy freeway, which leads from Houston toward San Antonio.

I like to eat these big, sloppy hamburgers with the mustard dripping on the scratched Formica tabletop, while I look out the window and watch all the maniacs in automobiles racing down the Katy, trying not to sideswipe each other.

Sometimes I wish I were like Lorna. It would certainly please my proper parents and my ultraproper grandmother. Lorna is what they call "outgoing" and always seems to know the right things to say. I've never seen Lorna fall over a chair, or trip over her own feet.

I tend to keep things all bottled up inside me, things that bother me a lot. Maybe too many things bother me, because they get into a muddle, and I don't really know what I want or where I'm going. Lorna and I haven't got a thing in common except that we seem to need each other and have since we met in the first grade and I was afraid to answer when the teacher called my name; and Lorna answered for me, because she had read my name on my lunch box and knew who I was.

I look at my watch, wondering where Lorna is. We drive over here in our separate cars, and she's usually right behind me.

A woman is coming in the door. Funny how she doesn't move in and grab a table, the way the regular customers do. She just stands there, watching Zack with a question in her eyes. He nods, and she looks at me and walks toward my table. What does she want? I've never seen her before. Well, maybe I have, but she just didn't register. She's one of those plump, average-looking women with a bad complexion, a woman no one would ever notice once, let alone twice. She's dressed in standard jeans and a light blue, short-sleeved T-shirt. It has a smooth, folded look, as though it had just been purchased.

She pulls out a chair and sits down, her hands trembling. Weird.

"I'm waiting for a friend," I tell her. "This is our table." She leans toward me confidentially. She clears her throat, but she doesn't say anything.

I find myself leaning toward her and speaking quietly, adopting her attitude. "What do you want?" I ask her.

"I'll be right with you," Zack calls from the counter. His friends turn, and their eyes slide over us, except for the big-shouldered black guy, who just stares straight ahead. I wonder what kind of jobs these men have. They always seem to be free to hang around his hamburger place on Friday afternoons. For all I know, maybe they've wondered the same thing about Lorna and me.

"I don't know what's on your mind," I tell the woman, "but a friend is coming to join me any minute and…"

A flicker of a smile moves across her face so quickly that I wonder if I saw it. She still doesn't speak, and she keeps twisting her fingers together so hard I imagine it must hurt.

Zack swings a leg over the nearest chair back and sits down at my table, too.

"What is this?" I ask him.

"You're Christina Lattimore, right?" he asks in a low voice.

I don't like people intruding in my life, disrupting things, especially these people; so I get as cold as the nose on the stone dog that sits by the gate in front of my grandmother's home in River Oaks and say, "I beg your pardon, but I see no reason to answer that question."

"Okay, okay," he says, still bending toward me, still talking in that low voice. "This here is my wife, Loretta. You come in this place every Friday. We just thought we'd get acquainted, that's all."

I automatically nod politely toward his wife. "I really am waiting for a friend, if you don't mind."

Zack stands up, scraping his chair back noisily, and pulls on the woman's arm. Her chair falls over with a clatter, and this time everyone in the place stares at us.

"Okay, okay, whatever you say," he answers, loud enough for people to hear.

What's on his mind, anyway? Why is he acting so strangely? There has to be a purpose in this, but for the life of me I can't figure out what it is. I feel as though I were in the middle of one of those audience-participation dramas little Mr. Bleims is always putting on in the drama department.

Zack walks back to the counter, and the woman scurries out the door, huddled into herself like a small brown field mouse. Lorna passes her in the doorway. What a relief. She is hurrying, but I'm the only one who would realize it. She isn't the least out of breath, and every hair is in place.

She puts her books down gracefully and glides into the chair next to mine.

"Something crazy is going on," I tell her.

"You mean the phone call? You know about it?"

"What phone call?"

"Well...you said something crazy was going on, and I thought you meant the phone call."

"You haven't told me *what* phone call. I don't know what you're talking about."

She settles herself with a little flutter and says, "Well, just as my last class was over, I got a note saying that I was to go to the office to accept a phone call."

"Who was it?"

"Nobody," she says. "It was the oddest thing. The operator kept trying to get the person who was placing the call, and kept telling me to hold. Finally she said there had been a mistake, and the call was for someone at a different number."

"Weird."

"I know. That's why when you said something was crazy, I thought you meant that phone call. So, anyhow, that's why I'm late." She sniffs the air and makes a puckery face. "I think I'll order mine without onions today."

I shrug. "I'll get them."

Zack has the hamburgers ready by the time I get to the counter. "No onions on one," I tell him.

He lifts the lid on one of the oversize buns, scrapes the glistening scramble of limp onion slices into a pan, slaps the top of the bun back on, and hands me a tray with the two burgers and Cokes on it. I put some money into his hand, and he gives me the change. Neither of us says another word to the other, but he looks at me again, knowingly. I'm really disturbed. I turn quickly so I don't have to look at him, and go back to the table.

"I don't think we should come in here anymore," I tell Lorna.

She takes a dainty bite of her burger. As usual I'm getting mustard on my nose, and a dill-pickle slice is spewing out of the top of the bun.

"Frankly," she says, "I'm glad. What made you change your mind?"

I start to tell her about Zack and his wife and the strange way they acted, but somehow it seems unimportant now, unreal, and the whole thing makes me uncomfortable to think about. So I just say, "Oh, the guy at the counter—that Zack—is creepy."

"I always thought so," she says. She sips her Coke.

"So next Friday let's go someplace else."

Lorna smiles. "Chris, why don't we go to Sakowitz's tearoom?"

They don't have mustard burgers in Sakowitz's tearoom, but Lorna has been patient with me for a long time. It's only fair that I do things her way for a while. I take a big bite, and mumble with my mouth full, "Okay."

"What did your parents say about the Summer-in-France program that Madame DeJon is planning?" Lorna asks.

This is a sore point with me. I clutch my feelings to myself, as though there were another hand inside of me, holding tightly. I try to shrug it off. "I'm just about to give up asking. I guess I'm the only one who won't be taking the trip."

Lorna looks up, immediately sympathetic. "But it's going to be so much fun," she says.

"I know. It's just that...well, I wish Madame DeJon hadn't arranged the whole thing around the study of the old cathedrals and Roman Catholic art. It turned my father off."

I pull a stiff napkin out of the chrome holder in the middle of the table and wipe my face. The napkin scratches my cheeks, but at least it cleans the mustard off my nose.

I can see Lorna searching for a comforting thing to say. "It's really very nice that your father is so religious in his own church," she offers.

"Is he?" I ask.

"Why, Chris, you know he is!" Lorna is puzzled. She has a funny expression on her face, as though she thinks I might be kidding but isn't sure. "I mean, look at how much time he gives to your church, going to those meetings in Washington and Hawaii and all those other places, and being a lay preacher and all that."

I just nod. I used to admire him, too, when I was little. I was always so proud when my father would hold me on his lap and show me another picture of himself in the newspaper because he had just spoken at a national assembly of churches, or vacationed with a famous church leader, or something like that. I used to be crazy about my father and love his stories and the deep vibrations in his chest as he sang to me, all curled into a secure ball on his lap.

But I have grown to see things differently. My father has a wispy, spindly secretary, Rosella, who looks up all the Bible quotations and writes his speeches in a small cubbyhole off his office in our house. And he stands up and gets praised for being a biblical authority and for his loving smile. It keeps him from having to show up at the office—where he doesn't know whether he's coming or going. And it keeps him away from my grandmother, who runs her family and her business with a strong hand.

My grandfather made the oil money and founded the company, and my grandmother operates it with terrific efficiency. My father is a vice president and collects a lovely salary. He has a fantastic house in the best section of Memorial. He also spends most of his time being a highly respected lay preacher. It's the best cop-out I can think of for not going to work.

"Maybe your father would change his mind if you pointed out to him that the study of cathedrals and art shouldn't bother him, because the whole world is more ecumenical now, and Catholics all over the United States even voted for a Baptist president," Lorna says.

"He's old guard," I tell her. "He hasn't reached that point of thought yet."

"Could your grandmother help change his mind?"

I think about this for a minute. "Maybe she could. I don't know."

"Why don't you ask her?"

A thought hits me, and I sit up straighter. "Listen, Lorna, I just remembered my trust fund. My grandfather set it up for me, and my grandmother holds the strings on it. But it's supposed to provide for my college and other study, and all that stuff. A trip like that's supposed to be educational. That's what it says in Madame DeJon's brochure."

"It's sort of like the old-fashioned idea of sending a girl through Europe before sending her off to college," Lorna says. "And you'd be in college in a year and a half."

I'm growing enthusiastic. "Right! And my grandmother might just go for that! And if I'm using my own money, and she talks to my father...You know he does anything she tells him to do."

Lorna actually clasps her hands as she smiles. "Oh, I'm so excited! I'm so glad you thought of it! When are you going to ask your grandmother?"

I look at my watch. "She winds things up early on Fridays. I could go over to her office now, and I bet she'd see me."

Lorna and I leave the hamburger place and walk to the parking lot. We talk about a lot of stuff, like getting together tonight and how I'm supposed to call her the minute I leave my grandmother's office. I get in my blue Cutlass and pull out into the traffic on the access road, heading for downtown Houston.

I'm sort of named after my grandmother, Cristabel Lattimore. But that's about the only thing we have in common—the first syllable in our given names.

They didn't give me her actual name, because everyone felt there could be only one Cristabel Lattimore. She's something of a legend in Houston, taking over the oil company when her husband died and making it grow twice as fast under her direction. She has a hand in Texas politics and local theater and regional art scholarships, and shows up all the time either in the society columns of the newspapers or on the business pages.

Once, when I was in second grade, I had a friend whose grandmother baked chocolate-chip cookies and told funny stories while she held us on her lap. I got so jealous of my friend that I stopped going to her house to play. I had only one grandmother nearby, and she never had that kind of lap.

I park the car in one of the slots Cristabel reserves for visitors, and take the elevator from the parking basement up to the thirty-fifth floor. The doors open without a sound, and I step onto a carpet that softly bounces me along, step-by-step, to the receptionist's desk.

The prim woman behind the desk smiles graciously at me and almost whispers, "I'll ring your grandmother, Christina." My grandmother spent I don't know how many hours when I was little drilling into me "A lady does not raise her voice, Christina." She must have gotten to her receptionist, too. The muted silence in this place used to make me feel reverent. Now it makes me want to break the spell and shout. Maybe because Cristabel has been a woman executive during a time in which they were an oddity, she is extremely careful about appearances. No one is allowed to spoil her public image.

The receptionist murmurs into the speaker on her desk, and an answering murmur floats back. "You may go in now," she says.

"Thank you," I say quietly.

My grandmother rises behind her desk as I come in, and offers me her cheek to kiss. She looks positively beautiful, as always. I don't know whether she uses color on her dark brown hair or not. I have the feeling she simply refused to let it go gray, and it obeyed her. She is dressed in a smart gray flannel suit and a coral blouse, and I think I'd like an outfit like that as a change from the stupid blue plaid skirt and blazer we have to wear through the entire twelve years at Madame Dejon's.

Twice a year my grandmother's secretary phones someone at Neiman Marcus and makes an appointment for her. Cristabel arrives punctually and is shown into a huge private dressing room, which has been reserved with her name on the door. Then a selection of dresses, suits, shoes, bags—everything she could possibly wear for the next six months— is brought in for her to try. She makes up her mind right away, her new wardrobe is charged and delivered, and at the end of the month her secretary pays the bill. Just like that. Cristabel thinks it's efficient. I think it's dull. I'd rather spend all day with Lorna, trying to find just the right pair of faded jeans.

"Hello, Cristabel," I say. She doesn't like to be called "Grandmother." I just call her that in my mind and when I'm talking about her to my friends. If I didn't think about Cristabel as my grandmother, I probably wouldn't think about her at all. The idea makes me shiver.

"Sit down, Christina," Cristabel says, and she slides into her huge leather executive chair.

I sink back into a soft, pale gold chair and look through the wide expanse of tinted glass over the city of Houston.

"You've got such a beautiful view, Cristabel," I say. "Why don't you turn your desk around so you can see it? You've always got your back to it."

She smiles. "I'm afraid I would only be distracted, Christina. It would be difficult to get all my work done and stare out the window, too." She taps a pencil against the gigantic blotter on her desk. "Is this a social visit, or is there something that you need?"

"A little of both," I tell her. "I haven't seen you for weeks, and I also want to ask you about something."

"And that something might concern a study program in France?"

I blink. "How did you know?"

"Your father told me that you were unhappy with his decision not to let you go."

"Cristabel," I say, "practically everyone in the junior class is going. It's...well, it's educational, and..." I remember what Lorna and I planned for me to say. "It's like the trips to Europe that girls used to take before they began college. Very...uh...traditional."

"I think," Cristabel says, "we had better keep this matter between you and your father."

I feel tears pounding behind my eyes. Tears can hurt, and I'm hurting. "My father is a religious bigot," I tell her.

She keeps her cool, poised look, but there is a quick flicker of her eyelashes. "Christina, your father not only has strong religious convictions, but he preaches them. He has a public image. If the course of study were broader, I'm sure he would allow you to go. Unfortunately, the fact that the study will be totally concerned with the art history of the Roman Catholic faith does bother him."

"I'm not an extension of my father! I'm a person with my own rights!" I lean forward eagerly. "Cristabel, I don't even have to depend on my father for the money to take the trip. It's a study tour—right? And you could let me use some of my trust fund for the trip. It's very educational, and it isn't so expensive if you think that it lasts all summer, and when I came back, ready for my senior year, I'd be… well…so informed, so…knowledgeable about France…so…"

She lifts a hand imperiously and says, "Christina, when it comes to your trust fund, the answer is an unequivocal no."

"But it's for my education!"

"Your education, as I see fit. Remember, I control every cent of that trust fund and always will. Contrary to what you may think, I was not sent to Europe after graduation from high school. I worked as a secretary to help put myself through the university."

"You want me to get a job? Is that it?"

"You are raising your voice, Christina."

"Even if I get a part-time job, I can't earn enough money to take that trip!"

"This has gone beyond the point of discussion, Christina. There is no question of your getting a job. Your life, for the next few years, is under my direction, and it includes the proper schooling, and an eastern university, with graduate school, if we later decide that your course of study warrants it."

I stand up. "Oh, Grandmother! Cristabel, I mean!" I catch myself quickly. "I don't know why you put that money aside for me if you won't let me use it! And if you're keeping me from going to save face for my father—well, I don't think it's fair! Don't you understand how important this trip is to me?"

Cristabel stands, too, facing me across the desk. Her voice is even softer than usual, making my words seem like an embarrassing shout echoing from the pale walls. "You are still a child, Christina. At your age, how could you possibly know what is really important and what is not?"

"But I *do* know what's important!"

"Remember your manners, Christina," she says.

The hurt grows stronger. "How can you talk about manners, when you must know this means so much to me?"

"I hope you'll review this conversation later and think about how selfish you sound," she says.

The words hit me. Selfish? What is selfish? My father lives in a beautiful house with eighteen rooms and doesn't know beans about the company in which he's vice president. I ask to use part of my own trust fund so that I can go with the rest of my class on a tour of France, and I'm selfish! I don't understand what my grandmother is talking about. I don't understand my parents. I don't understand anything.

I turn and run out of the office. I wish I had enough courage to slam the door, but I don't. I am crying now, and I don't want anyone to see me, so I charge into the waiting elevator and sniffle, trying to fish in my handbag for something to wipe my nose on. There is nothing left of the packet of tissues except the wrapper.

When I get home, I'll have to call Lorna and tell her that as far as the trip to France goes, I'm out. I'm furious with my grandmother! I'm furious with my stupid father. I'm furious with the whole stupid world I live in.

[TWO]

WHEN I get home, I remember to leave my Cutlass on the circular drive in front of the house instead of putting it away. I'll be going to Lorna's later.

It's quiet here, away from the noise of the main streets. I stand still for a moment, aware of the early daffodil buds that look ready to pop open, and the tiny leaves sprouting on the Chinese tallow trees. A jay squawks at me and sails off in a streak of blue. It's March, and spring comes early in Houston, after a wet, cold winter.

For a moment I've been distracted, and I'm glad. I have stopped being angry at Cristabel. What difference does it make? What difference does anything make? Somehow either I always care an awful lot about something, or else I don't care at all—like being dead inside and not knowing what to do about it. I don't understand myself. I wish I did.

There is a small dark green car parked on the street down near the garages. Probably belongs to Della or one of her friends. This is Friday, the night she leaves early. Della always lives it up on Fridays, and goes around Saturday mornings as if her head were in a basket. She tells me how she dances, and her eyes light up. She says she can sling it around better than the best of them, although I can't picture those two-hundred-plus pounds slinging their way around a dance floor. I guess that inside all that Della there is a foxy chick who comes out on Friday nights.

I run up the broad steps to the veranda and put my key in the front-door lock. There is some resistance, and I bend over to look closer. The door is unlocked, and there is a small piece of that invisible cellophane tape over the side, to keep the lock from closing. Why? Who put it there?

We're all careful to keep the doors in the

house locked, because there are plenty of kiddie pot heads around these neighborhoods who'll steal anything to get a few dollars to buy grass.

The tape on the door is weird, and I am suddenly alert, with a shivery feeling at the back of my neck. Is someone in our house who shouldn't be here? Could someone be casing the house? I've got to find out.

I open the door, leaving the tape in place, and call at the top of my lungs, "Della! Mother! Anyone there?"

The late-afternoon sunlight is streaming through the fanlight over the door, creating a prismatic effect with the crystal chandelier that hangs in the entry hall, splashing tiny rainbows of color over the white marble tiles and the bowl of white porcelain roses in the vase under the nearly life-size wedding portrait of my parents. It looks like a spot for warmth and peace, but that's not the way I feel.

"Della! Where are you?" I screech.

"Good God Almighty! You trying to scare me to death?" Della's face peers at me over the banister at the top of the curving staircase.

"Della, are you all right? Is everything all right?"

"Of course it is. What's the matter with you?"

"It's this door. I've got to show you something."

"Not right this minute," she says. "I've got to get these sheets and towels put away. Y'all come up here if you want to talk." Her face disappears.

I take the stairs two at a time and run down the hall to the linen closet, where Della is putting sheets in neat stacks with sachet bags tucked between them, the way my mother likes them. I quickly tell her about the door.

For the first time she straightens and looks at me. "That's crazy," she says. "I've been here all day. Rosella and your mama and daddy have been in and out, but that's all."

"You didn't hear anyone trying to get in?"

"Anyone wants to get in is going to get in. Why put some of that tape on the door?"

"I don't know," I tell her. "That's what I'm trying to find out. You're sure no one was here at all—not even a salesman?"

There is a sudden awareness in Della's eyes. "There was a woman," she says. Then she shrugs. "But she was just looking for a house number, and I gave it to her, and she stayed outside the whole time."

"Tell me about it."

"There's nothing much to tell. She just came to the door and said she was trying to find somebody's house number—darned if I can remember the name—and I went to the phone book and looked it up and wrote it down for her. Then I just came back and gave her the paper, and she thanked me and went away."

"But did you leave the door open?"

"Of course I didn't. You think I'm witless? When I went for the address, I shut the door like always."

"How long ago was this?"

"I don't know. Maybe an hour. About that, I guess."

"What kind of car did the woman have?"

Della shuts the wide doors of the linen closet. She frowns, thinking hard. "I don't remember seeing a car," she says.

"Della," I tell her. "Come with me right away. I have to show you that door!"

"Okay, okay!" She puffs along after me as I race back down the stairs.

The door is shut, as I left it. I take hold of the doorknob to open it, but it doesn't budge.

"There's something crazy here!" I tell her. I turn the knob, and the door swings inward. The tape that held the lock back is gone!

Della looks at the door lock and back at me. The frown is deep on her forehead. "Where's this tape you were talking about?"

"It's gone," I say. I'm trying to figure this out, and for a minute my mind is blank.

Della suddenly relaxes, puts her hands on her hips, and shakes her head at me. "Now I understand," she says. "I was telling you about that movie I saw on late TV—the one about the cat burglar, and it scared me so much I couldn't sleep. You're playing a prank on me, Christina."

Her reaction startles me almost as much as finding the tape on the door. She doesn't believe me. "Della, I'm telling you the truth. I'm not playing pranks or trying to scare you. When I got home, there was a piece of tape on this door, keeping the lock from closing. Really there was!"

"Then where did the tape go?"

I search for the answer, and it hits me so hard that it makes me gasp for breath. "Della!" I say. "I went upstairs to talk to you and left the front door unguarded. Whoever put the tape on the lock was still in the house somewhere! When he left, he took the tape off! Do you realize that all the time we were talking upstairs there was someone down here?" My voice has risen to a squeak, and Della reaches over to grip my shoulders, shaking me a little.

"Calm down," she says. "If there was anybody in this house, then we would have heard them."

"Not if they were quiet," I say. "That woman who came to the door—she could have put the tape on while you were talking to her. Did you see her hold on to the edge of the door?"

Della thinks. The blue jay scolds loudly just outside the door, and I want to shout at it, "Be quiet! Go away! We're trying to work something out!" I feel somewhat irrational. I have to know who was in our house and why.

"Maybe she did," Della says. "Maybe not. She did lean over to look inside the hallway and say how pretty it was."

"And she held on to the edge of the door to support herself?"

"Might be." Della sighs. "I just can't remember."

I step outside and lean in. Automatically I grab the edge of the door to hold. And the place where it's logical to hold is at the lock, in the middle of the door edge. "Did she do it like this?" I ask Della.

"Might be," Della says.

I glance down the street. The small green car is gone. What would a woman want in our house? Was she trying to steal something?

"We're going to have to look around and see if anything is stolen," I tell Della. "Maybe we should call the police."

She quickly says, "Not until we find out if something is gone!"

I remember that when Della came to work here two years ago she told me that her son, by her first husband, was in prison for armed robbery. When the police came for him, he was in Della's house, and things got pretty scary for a while. Della got busted herself once, when the police broke up a poker game she was in. She isn't too crazy about having anything to do with the police.

"All right. You and I will look through the house," I say. "You see if she took a radio or TV set or anything obvious that she could carry. I'll look in my father's office."

"No need to look upstairs," Della says. "I've been up there ever since she came to the door."

I go into my father's office. He doesn't have a safe. He keeps his money in the bank and uses checks or credit cards for almost everything. They couldn't be after his money. I look around his office, which I'm sure doesn't look like any other man's office. There are books against one wall, and they are all religious and psychology books, many of them reference books, which Rosella uses to write his speeches. There is a window overlooking the veranda, and a door on the far side that opens into Rosella's little office. The rest of the wall space is covered with pictures of my father. In all the photos he is either giving a speech or getting an award. Even the picture on his desk is a photo of himself, in living color, instead of the traditional picture of his wife. He's a tall man, beginning to bald, but still handsome. Although he looks like Cristabel, he's not a carbon copy of his mother. She has a vitality that my father will never have.

My mother and father are obsessed with photographs of themselves, which they hang in every room of the house. There used to be more, but my grandmother tactfully told them the decor would be improved with some good paintings instead, so my mother hired an art dealer in New York to go to Europe to purchase some old masters. Now a few rather dark paintings hang on some of the walls. Two of them are incredibly ugly. I think my mother got taken.

Nothing on the desk or anywhere in the room seems to have been disturbed. I don't want to go through my father's desk. I'll tell him about the woman when he gets home, and he can look through it himself. I walk into Rosella's cubbyhole, but there is nothing in the room except her small desk, a typewriter, a lamp, and tidy stacks of papers. There would be nothing to steal in here.

I go through the library and the sunroom,

then meet Della face-to-face as I enter the dining room. We both jump.

"You've made me so nervous I'm late starting dinner," she complains. "And I sure can't find any sign of anyone being in here."

"Neither can I."

"Your mama and daddy will be home pretty soon. They went to a meeting of that United Church something or other. You tell them about it when they get home, and they'll know what to do. I got to get dinner started."

I go upstairs to my room and throw my blazer on the bed. I think about reading that essay for my English class, but I've left my books in my car. So I sit at my dressing table and brush my hair. It's long and dark and straight. I wish it weren't straight. I ought to wear blue eye shadow. It would bring out the color of my eyes. I don't think Della believes me. Maybe my parents won't believe me either. But I know I saw that tape! I didn't imagine it. That woman had to be in our house. Then she took the tape off the door and left before we got downstairs again. That's how it had to be, unless I'm going crazy.

Am I going crazy? No. It's an interesting thought, but I don't think so. I wonder if I should use a blue eyeliner, too. There's a little red spot on my nose. It's going to get huge and ugly before it goes away. Blast! Who was that woman?

I hear voices downstairs, so I drop my hairbrush on the dressing table and straighten my skirt. My blouse is wrinkled. It always looks wrinkled, even when it's fresh from the laundry. I don't know what to do about it, though it upsets my mother.

She'd like me to hang up my blazer before I come down, and I almost do, reacting automatically; but then I decide the heck with it. The blazer is out of place on the little-girl, frilly, pink-canopied bed. The room is not me. The interior decorator liked pink ruffles and dressing-table skirts, and my mother loves it. I just live here.

By the time I get downstairs, my mother and father have been talking to Della. Rosella is with them. They all have identical expressions on their faces as they watch me come down the stairs. It reminds me of the way they looked at me when I threw up at my seventh birthday party and they couldn't believe I would do such a thing.

"Della believes that you're playing a prank on her, Christina," my father says.

"When I came home, there was tape on the door, holding the lock open. It's true. Believe me."

I jump down the last two steps, which causes my mother to wince. "We believe you, dear," she says. "It's just that Della says you both searched the house, and nothing had been taken."

"Nothing obvious," I tell her. "I didn't look inside Daddy's desk. The woman was downstairs, not upstairs, since Della would have seen her if she went upstairs; so she must have wanted something in Daddy's desk. I wish you'd look through it. I really do."

My father nods. "I'll look right away, although I have little in that desk that anyone would want."

"Any money?"

"Maybe twenty dollars or so. No more than that."

My mother and I follow him into his office. Rosella skitters along behind us.

My father goes straight to the desk and opens the top drawer. Then he looks up at me. "The money is right here. If that woman had gone through the desk looking for things, she surely would have taken the money, don't you think?"

"But then what did she want?"

Rosella has gone to check her office. She comes back shaking her head. "No one has been in there."

My mother sinks into the brown leather chair near the door. "We had better look at the information we have. We keep talking about a 'she' person who has taken something from the house. But did you actually see some woman in here, Christina?"

"Well...no."

"Did you even hear anyone in the house?"

"No, I didn't."

"So all we know for sure is that there was a piece of cellophane tape on the door lock when you came home, and it was not there when you brought Della to see it."

I give a long, elaborate sigh. What is the matter with the whole world? I'm not the only one in it who is all mixed up. Everyone's mixed up. Nothing is right. Nothing is normal. I saw the tape. It held the lock open. That's all I know, except that it sounds like a crazy story in retrospect. My parents believe me, but Della looked as though she thought I was lying.

"Never mind," I tell them. "I don't understand anything about the piece of tape, so we might as well forget it."

My mother shrugs. "I suppose that's a good idea. We'll forget about it for now. Let's see if Della is ready to serve dinner."

We follow her to the dining room. No one invites Rosella to stay for dinner. It's just taken for granted that if she is here she eats with us. She and my father keep strange hours, because he often wants to work in the evening. Rosella doesn't have a family. She lives all alone in an apartment somewhere. I don't even know where. I don't think about Rosella much. She's a small-boned woman with a little pointy nose and eyes that always seem to be asking questions. She doesn't talk a lot, and I guess that makes me uncomfortable. People like me, who keep their feelings inside, never feel at ease with others who do the same. It's sort of like two icebergs keeping their distance from each other, never knowing when all that hidden stuff is going to collide.

We seat ourselves at the table, and my father gives his usual long, involved blessing in the pear-shaped tones that have helped him find recognition as a lay preacher. While he is praying, I examine the bowl of pebbles and bulbs in the center of the table. The bulbs have sprouted bright green tops, and they push through the pebbles.

I realize my father has stopped speaking, so I quickly say, "Amen," and lift my head. My mother helps herself to a chicken casserole and passes it to Rosella, who passes it to me.

"Did you have a nice day, Christina?" my mother asks. "I suppose you and Lorna went to that dreadful hamburger place you usually go to?"

"I had a pits day," I say. "Nothing went right."

She sighs, and before she can tell me I shouldn't say "pits," I add, "I went to see Cristabel today."

"How nice," she says. "It was thoughtful of you to visit your grandmother."

"I went to see her about using some

money from my trust fund to take that summer study program with Madame DeJon," I say. "She wouldn't let me touch it."

My father stares at me. "I told you I didn't want you to take that course," he says. "I'm tired of hearing about it. That's all you've talked about for weeks."

"I know how you feel about all of this being tied in with the Catholic religion," I say. "I thought Cristabel could help me talk you into it. I think I'm the only one in the junior class who isn't going."

I don't like subterfuge. I don't like pretending things with people. I don't bother to talk about most things with my parents because they don't really understand. But when I do want to talk about something, I say it straight out. I imagine that by this time they're used to me.

"What did your grandmother say?" Cristabel always makes my father nervous. I just wish she had been on my side.

"She said she wouldn't release any of the money."

"Good. I should have known she would agree with me."

"But I don't agree!" I said. "And I told her so! I think I should go, since my whole class is going! I don't want to be left out!"

My mother leans toward me. I hope she is going to offer me some support—sympathy, at least—but she says, "Oh, Christina, I do hope you weren't rude to Cristabel!"

"I didn't try to be rude," I say, "but she does know I was upset."

"It would be so foolish to be rude," my mother says. "Your grandmother has done so much for us." She doesn't say it, but the meaning hangs in the air: *and will continue to do so much for us if you play the game by behaving yourself.*

"We've discussed that trip enough," my father says. "You may think that my religious feelings are old-fashioned, but I must abide by my principles." He leisurely butters a roll as though it's the most important thing he could be doing. "Suppose we change the subject."

My mother puts on her bright, conversational face and says, "Christina, did you know that Rosella is going to visit her mother next week? Her mother has been ill."

I blink at Rosella, trying to remember

where her mother lives. It's hard enough to picture Rosella with a mother.

"She lives in Chicago," Rosella says, as though she can read my mind. "I'll be flying direct to Chicago from Houston on Monday evening."

"That's nice," I say. I'm sure there are other things I should babble about, like what is the matter with her mother, and all that, but the pause becomes too long, and anything I think of now would sound awkward.

Finally my father begins to talk to my mother about a lecturer who might be invited to Houston for an important seminar.

Rosella makes appropriate little noises of approval, but darts occasional glances at me. I can see she doesn't believe me about the door and is trying to figure out what that was all about. I wish she wouldn't be so obvious about her feelings.

I tune out my father and Rosella and concentrate on finishing dinner. I must get over to Lorna's house. I hadn't called her in all the commotion, and I feel like talking to her. I'm glad I have a friend like Lorna. I've never wanted many friends. I'm happy to have Lorna for all the deep and close stuff, and a few others who like to do things when we all want to go somewhere and have fun.

I wait for a pause, then break in. "May I please be excused?"

I am pushing my chair back from the table when my mother asks, "Do you have plans for tonight, dear? Do you have a date?"

"A date?" I'm surprised that she'd ask. "Where am I going to meet any guys in a school for girls?"

"Now, Christina, you know good and well that some of those girls have brothers who could be interested in you. Just a few weeks ago you went out with Sally Jaster's brother. Sally said he thought you were terrific, and I'm surprised he didn't call back and ask for another date."

"He did," I say, "but I turned him down."

Her mouth is a little O. "Why would you do that?"

"Because he's a drunken slob."

"Oh, come now, Christina! The Jasters are prominent people in town."

"That doesn't keep their charming son

from getting drunk and practically throwing up in my lap."

"What?"

"Well, he would have, except when he started gagging I pushed him out his side of the car. And then when he finished, I helped him crawl back in on the passenger side and drove him home."

"You didn't tell us any of this," my father says.

"I didn't think it was important."

"But surely we should know if something unfortunate happens to our daughter when she's out on a date."

"I don't think so," I say. "Then you'd just worry the next time I went out. And it's over, so who cares?"

"Oh, my," my mother says. My father doesn't say anything.

"May I please be excused?" I repeat. "I want to go over to Lorna's and play music."

"All right," my father says. "Just don't be home too late."

"Meaning before midnight."

"That's it."

I'd probably argue about my curfew time, except that I've argued enough for today. I'm tired of it. I suppose I'll be glad enough to go to bed at midnight, instead of later, but it's the last thing I'd let my parents know.

I change into my old jeans and a rugby shirt and pull on an old white sweater. I cut through the kitchen on the way to the driveway. Della is just finishing up, and I ask, "Would you like a lift to the bus stop?"

"No thanks," she says, wiping her hands on a dish towel. "I got someone coming to get me."

"Big date, huh?" I grin at her.

But she shakes her head. "You run along now. Have fun."

"You, too," I answer. In a few moments I'm headed for Lorna's. I don't have far to go, but as I drive through the traffic on Memorial Drive I think a car is following me. I turn off on Lorna's street, and no one else turns. I guess I'm getting spooked or something. No one was following me.

I pull up in front of Lorna's house, the porch light a bright orange spot among the slender pin oaks that grow thickly on the front lawn. Lorna's mother went in for modern decor on the inside, and their whole house is done in tones of rust, gray, white, and black. It's the kind of thing that makes you think "Fantastic" when you first see it, but after a while you find yourself wishing someone would come in with a can of green paint, or blue...anything to break the monotony.

Lorna's parents go out a lot, because they get involved in causes and seminars and all sorts of things. Right now it's a marriage encounter group, and they are so wrapped up in all this new thought that they practically ignore Lorna. Lorna behaves very well about it. She says she's a stoic. Tonight her parents have already left for a party, and we have the house to ourselves, so we turn on the stereo at top volume.

The music gets so loud that a small print of a lion shudders and falls off the wall. It doesn't matter because the glass doesn't break. We'll put it back later.

"Why didn't you call me?" Lorna asks.

"I couldn't. When I got home, we thought we had a burglar, and that kept me busy until my parents got home and we had dinner."

Lorna looks at me with wide eyes. "What should I ask first? Did you have a burglar? Or what did your grandmother say?"

"No," I tell her. "No, in both cases."

"Oh, Christina!" Lorna says. "I wanted you to go to France on that study program. It won't be the same without you! Is there no hope?"

"No hope," I say. Sometimes Lorna talks like one of the Victorian Gothics she likes to read. "I wish I were independent and had my own money and could do what I wanted without asking my father's permission."

I don't want to let Lorna know how upset I really feel, so I quickly say, "Let's talk about something else. Did you get that new Top Hits CD?"

"Yesterday," Lorna says. "But tell me the rest. Tell me about your burglar."

"It wasn't a burglar. It wasn't anybody. I came home and the front door wasn't locked. There was a piece of invisible cellophane tape over the lock. So I ran in to find out what had happened, and went upstairs to talk to Della. When we came down, the tape was gone and the door was locked."

"You're kidding!"

"No, really. Don't ask me to explain about the tape, because we looked all over downstairs, and nothing was missing. And we didn't see anybody. The only person who had come to the house was a woman who asked Della to look up an address."

"Could *she* have done it?"

"Yes, I think she could. What I don't know is why, since nothing was missing."

"That's wild."

Lorna puts on the new CD, and we listen for a while. I am still fighting the desperate mood. The room smells like upholstery cleaner and stale ashtrays, and that depresses me even more.

"Lorna," I ask, "what's important?"

"Important?" Lorna echoes, looking puzzled.

"You know what I mean. Sometimes I think I really need something in my life, and then it turns out not to be important at all. Sometimes it works the other way. So how do you figure out what is really important and what isn't?"

"I don't know," Lorna says. "Maybe if it has to do with love, it's important."

"Then school wouldn't be there at all, and yet adults keep telling us that classes and grades and homework and all that are the most important things in our lives. I wonder if it means more to them than it does to us."

"I think what's most important to my father is how much money he makes," she says.

"My father likes money, too," I say. "But it's always there, so he takes it for granted. I think the most important thing to my father is…"

"His religion," Lorna answers for me.

"No," I say slowly. "I think the religion is a means to an end. It's a way to make him somebody in his own right, a way that's different from his mother's way, the only thing in his life over which his mother doesn't have control."

"What's important to you?" Lorna asks.

I groan. "That's what I don't know yet. And I don't know how to rate things to find out."

"Maybe we could make a scale of one to ten," Lorna says.

"Except the scale would keep changing, and then the things that were important one day wouldn't be the next. Remember how it was when we were little? How we just had to go to a birthday party or ice-skating or some-thing like that?"

"Yes. I see where you're coming from."

"Right now I want to get enough money to go on that trip to France. How long is that going to seem important?"

"I thought you didn't want to talk about it."

"I don't." I get up and stretch, then pull my shirt down where it clings over my ribs. "We're running out of time. I've got to be home by midnight or my father will have an attack. What have you got to eat around here?"

"Not much," Lorna says. "My mother put us all on a diet."

"Why don't we cook something? How about making fudge?"

She hesitates. "It's fattening."

"Good," I say. It strikes us both funny, and we start to giggle. The giggles become strident as we hunt up a recipe for fudge, improvise with cocoa when we can't find cooking choco-late in the kitchen, and drop the vanilla bottle into the bubbling brown mess in the pan.

"We went wrong somewhere," Lorna says, fishing out the now empty bottle of vanilla. "I don't think it's ever going to get thick."

"Then let's eat it with spoons!"

We pour the fudge into a bowl, and dip in and out of it with our spoons, burning our tongues, hopping around the kitchen, and laughing like maniacs.

Worst fudge I ever ate. I'm enjoying every minute of it.

Finally I look at the clock. "Uh-oh! I'd better get home in a hurry!"

"What'll we do with the rest of the fudge?" Lorna asks.

"Let's give it to someone we don't like," I answer, and this sets us off again with stomach-holding laughter.

Finally I put on my sweater and walk out to my car. I open the door, and light floods the darkness around me. Lorna waves, and closes and locks her door, flipping off the porch light.

The night is still, and the moon is just a useless sliver in a dark sky. I slide behind the wheel, automatically lock my door, and head home. Behind me a car starts, but I'm reliving the fun I had with Lorna, so I forget it, not paying much attention.

In a few minutes I pull into our driveway. I decide not to put the car in the garage. It's too lonely and dark there. I have a strong desire to get inside as quickly as possible. I leave the car on the drive, then fumble for a moment with my keys, dropping them once and fishing around in the dust until I find them. My fingers tremble and my breath comes in little, quick gasps.

Someone has stepped out of the bushes directly in front of me! It's too dark to see who it is. There is just a faint glimmer of light where two eyes should be in a dark mask. I open my mouth to yell, but a hand is clasped over it. I bite down hard...harder...on the finger that slips between my teeth. The taste is salty and bitter, and the hand stinks of sweat.

There is a muffled grunt from the person behind me. I try to kick, but the figure in front of me has grabbed my arm, twisting it painfully, and I feel the prick of a needle in my arm, near the elbow.

I remember the anesthetic I got when my wisdom teeth were pulled. I could actually feel it traveling up my arm in a straight, swift line toward my brain. That's what's happening to me now. I live through a sharp instant of fear. That's all I remember.

[THREE]

I AM HAVING crazy, wild dreams, with someone humming in a rhythm that pulses and fades. I am tired and I cling to sleep, although it is so intense that my mouth is dry and my eyelids itch.

I am thirsty, terribly thirsty, and I think I will open my eyes and wake up in a hospital bed with stiff, fresh sheets, and a nurse telling me that everything went fine while my wisdom teeth were removed, and I should spit out the blood in this little pan, dear.

But I open my eyes and the light is gray and grim. I realize I am lying on a cot in what looks like a cement-walled basement, with tiny windows at the top of the walls at ground level. I cry out for my mother, but the sleep is overpowering and I drift backward, dreaming that I called my mother's name.

I know it is much later when I can wake enough to force myself to sit up, dropping my legs over the side of the cot as though they were lead weights. My mouth is so dry that I want to gag, but there is a small table next to the cot, and a carafe of water and a glass are on it. I sip the water, remembering that it shouldn't be gulped, and try to force the mist from my mind so that I can think clearly about what has happened.

I splash some of the cold water on my face. It's cool in this basement, and I'm glad I have my sweater. I must think of what to do. I stand, but drop back on the cot. My knees wobble. I must not take this too fast.

The blanket on the cot is rough—army surplus—but I pull it around me and lean back against the wall. Last night. What happened last night?

The figure under the trees comes to mind again. I look into those dark eye sockets and begin to tremble. Sitting on the cot and realiz-

ing that I have been kidnapped, I am so terrified that I can't cry or scream or shout, held
by a fear that is so penetrating it shakes me,
the way a cat worries a field mouse before
killing it.

Is that what will happen to me? Will I be
killed?

The panic rises from the pit of my stomach. I jump to my feet, staggering, trying to
focus my eyes properly. There are narrow,
rough cement steps at the far end of this small
room, and they lead to a door. I am going to
climb those stairs and beat on that door and
scream until someone hears me!

But vomit comes up into my mouth. I look
around wildly and see an open door leading to
a small bathroom. I make it just in time, lean
over the toilet, and am very sick. There is a
small washbasin nearby, and after I flush the
toilet I wash my face, splashing it with water
over and over until I can think more clearly.

I'm glad I was sick. It kept me from making
contact with whoever is on the other side of
the door at the top of the stairs. I realize that
there were two people, maybe more. As my

head clears, I remember the scents of the night—the large sweaty hand over my mouth and the odor of fear. Fear has a taste and fear has a smell—bitter and gagging. It surprises me. I must remember to tell Lorna about it.

The thought surfaces that I may never see Lorna or my family again, and I begin to cry. Leaning against the rough wall and blowing my nose on a fistful of toilet paper, I cry until the tears give way to a series of long, shuddering sighs.

Then, for the first time, I can think. I decide that the best thing I can do is to become familiar with the room I am in. I walk around the small basement. Aside from the steps on the far wall and the cot table, there is a huge furnace with pipes extending upward into the basement ceiling, like giant arms. It's an old-fashioned furnace with a door in the side. It's not on, and there is no pilot light anywhere around it. Are the people who live in this house warm enough in the early spring not to use the heat? Or is this house so old that it has no regular inhabitants and the utilities are turned off?

There is one way to check. I see a light switch at the top of the stairs, and I climb them cautiously, my heart pounding. If someone should open the door, I don't know what I would do. Maybe I'd faint. I have never fainted, and don't know what it feels like, but I have an idea it's something I might do.

I flip on the switch. Nothing happens. The bulb in the single ceiling socket remains blank. So what does this tell me? Not much.

Discouraged, I go swiftly down the stairs again and walk around the room. A large, shiny tree roach scuttles across a corner and into a hole in the cement near the flooring. I shudder. Will the roaches come out at night when I'm asleep? And if there are no lights, will I be able to see them? My stomach heaves again, but I force back the nausea. I must keep a firm hold on my emotions and try to think clearly.

There is one thing this basement tells me. The house is an old one. Because of flooding problems, no basements or cellars have been built in Houston for many years. And it must be a big house to have a basement and bathroom down here. Old heating system, old basement. Where would I be? The Heights? West University? Or am I even in Houston? Maybe I was taken to another town or city. I have no idea what time of day it is. I don't even know what day it is. Could I have slept over into another day? I am totally disoriented.

My watch. I see that it hasn't stopped, although as I wind it, I find it was close to running down. All right. That gives me something solid. It's Saturday, no later, or my watch wouldn't be running.

Strange how I am comforted by a fact that seems so insignificant. It's just something to hang on to.

I sit on the side of the cot, again wrapping the rough blanket around my shoulders. Surprisingly, the blanket smells clean. I notice that the cheap muslin sheets have been ironed. Do people still iron sheets? The floor has been swept. The basement is very tidy, very plain, very blank. Nothing much to remember. But I am going to remember. I promise myself to remember every single detail about this place, about the people who brought me here. I am angry now. I am not going to die. I am not going to give in to them. I am going to help the police find them whenever I get out of here!

I sip some more water. I'm beginning to get hungry, and with the hunger grows the desire to meet my kidnappers face-to-face. They are not frightening beings any longer. They are people, and I want to know why they have brought me to this place.

I hear the muffed sound of a door closing upstairs and footsteps over my head. Have these people been in another part of the house? Or have they been out and are now returning? It's weird to hear steps over your head and not know whose they are. It's like living in a house with ghosts. I find myself whimpering. I take a deep breath. I must not let go!

There is the sound of a door being unlocked at the top of the stairs. I stiffen, every part of my body tense. It hurts to breathe.

A man dressed in jeans and a white T-shirt appears. He wears a black knit ski mask over his head. He turns and closes the door silently, then comes down the steps, deliberately, carefully. He carries a tray, and I can smell beef soup. My stomach lurches. I didn't know I was so terribly hungry.

I look into the slits of the ski mask. Pale eyes look back at me. I'm not as frightened now as I was when this person was an un-known. In a way he looks comical, like an over-grown kid on Halloween. Dumb.

He puts the tray on the table. There is a thin wedding band on his left hand, and a large bandage on his middle finger. So his was the hand I bit. Good! I hope it went through to the bone!

"Do you want to know why you're here?" he asks me.

I try to recognize the voice, but I can't. I think hard, so I don't answer his question. It makes him uncomfortable.

He speaks again, a little more loudly. "Lis-ten, girl, you got to do something."

Again I am silent, waiting for him to con-tinue.

He sounds angry now, and his hands move uneasily up and down the legs of his jeans. "I'm talking to you, girl! I've got instruc-tions for you!"

And now I realize where my power lies. If I am silent, I have a weapon against him—my only weapon. Before, I was only waiting to speak. Now I refuse to speak. I'll see what happens.

"Dammit!" he says. "Well, if you won't talk to me, then listen, because there is something you got to do." He walks nervously back and forth to the wall at the left, staring up at the windows, as though checking them. It is easy to see the nail heads that hold the windows tightly shut. There would be no way to climb out of those small windows anyway. My mind has somehow registered that, because I seem to have known it already.

There was no click of a lock when he shut that door. I can move faster than he can, I bet, since he's not expecting me to try anything. He's at the far wall. Maybe it would give me the chance I need. It's better than sitting here, wondering what will happen next. As his back is turned, I dash toward the door, stumbling up the stairs.

I'm almost at the top when he grabs my leg, slamming me down on my stomach on the steps. The pain makes me cry out. He pulls my legs, dragging me down the stairs. I can only tuck in my elbows close to my body and try to protect my face, thankful that my sweater covers my arms so they won't be cut by the rough cement. I am furious. I am filled with hate. If there were any way I could kill this man, I would. The thought scares me enough to bring me back to my senses, and the heat of hatred drains away.

I huddle at the bottom of the stairs until he speaks to me again.

"Get up and go back to that cot," he says.

I do as he tells me. I sit and face him, staring defiantly into those pale eyes.

"You're going to have to sign a letter to your grandmother," he says.

I shake my head.

He's disconcerted, and that gives me a tiny feeling of triumph. It's as though I've won a blow in our fight.

"Oh, yes, you will," he tells me. "Because that's the way we've planned it. You're going to sign the ransom note we typed, and I'm going to deliver it." When I don't respond, his voice becomes wheedling. "Look, girl, you haven't got anything to lose if you sign the letter. As soon as we get the money, we'll let you go."

I continue to stare at him.

"I'm not kidding," he says. "You'll have to sign the note if you want to get out of here!"

His eyes light on the tray, and he stands a little straighter. "If you want to eat, you'll have to write your name. No food for you until you do."

I am faster this time than he. I pick up the bowl of soup and throw it at him. That is my answer.

He stands there with the dark broth running down the front of his T-shirt, and he is too surprised to do anything but curse. Then he reaches out and cuffs me across the side of the head with his open hand. The force knocks me sideways, and I fall on the cot.

"Dammit! I didn't want to do that!" he shouts at me. "I'm not supposed to hit you! And you're supposed to write your name on the letter! That's how it's planned! Dammit!" He picks up the pieces of the broken bowl, puts them on the tray, and stomps up the stairs without another word.

I'm hungry! But I'm also satisfied with what I did. Maybe it was stupid, maybe not. Maybe he will come downstairs and kill me because I'm not following whatever plan he's got worked out. But I feel that for now I've won. I've had the best of him. My face stings from the slap, but I feel good inside. I'll have to give this more thought.

Always before in my life I've been able to plan things in advance, to make decisions. But suddenly I'm faced with a situation in which I have to play it as it goes, step-by-step. What if I make the wrong move?

What would my father do in a case like this? My mother?

I think my mother would dissolve completely. She's never had to face anything threatening in her life. But maybe I'm not giving her enough credit. I've never had anything threatening happen to me either until now. Will my children someday have any idea of what I'm like inside? Of how I think and what I'd do in a crisis? At the moment I feel close to my mother, and this surprises me. Since I was a very young child, my mother and I have not been demonstrative with each other. Is it because I feel so alone that I long to see her?

The cockroach ventures out once more, its feelers waving as it explores, looking for danger. Seeing none, it travels in a straight line to a shadow behind the heater.

I know what my father would do if he were here in my place. He would pray. I try to think of a prayer, but nothing forms in my mind except the word "please." That is not much of a prayer, but my mind is blank. I can't even remember the baby prayers I used to say at bedtime while my father listened. All that comes back to me is the line, "If I should die before I wake..." Forget it! That's not a thought I want to dwell on right now!

The room is getting dimmer, and I realize that it must be late afternoon. I am getting used to hearing footsteps over my head, and I try to sort them out. One set seems to be heavy, one a little lighter. Are two people there? More? I wish I knew.

My stomach is rumbling like a Honda. I wonder if they can hear it all the way upstairs. If I don't sign the note, I'll go without food. The body can live for a number of days without food, as long as it has water, and there is water from the faucet in the little bathroom. But if I go without food for too long, I will lose my strength. I might need all the strength I have to get away from these people. There is no way to know.

From what the man said, the letter is already typed and I'm just supposed to sign my name. If they'd let me write it, maybe I could work in some message to Cristabel so she wouldn't give them the money. I don't want these kidnappers to get money from my grandmother! The whole idea of their using me to take her money makes me angry again.

The door opens. This time I'm ready for him. I sit very still as he comes down the stairs. He's carrying a pad with a sheet of paper on it, and a pencil. No food.

He comes to stand directly in front of me, and I must look up at him. "Are you ready to sign your name to this letter?" he asks. His voice is angry.

I nod my head, indicating yes, I am ready, and he seems startled. Good. I have caught him off balance a second time.

"Oh. Well, all right then," he says. He hands me the pad and pencil.

I begin to read the letter, and I gasp. It begins, "Dear Cristabel"!

He laughs, his ego feeding the words. "I'm a smart guy. I know all about you, girl. I know that's what you call your grandmother."

I am trying to think this out when he says, "Come on. Speed it up. What are you doing?"

I merely glance up at the man, waiting, until he says, "Okay. Read the damn thing if you've got to."

It's a short, simple letter that sounds like something from an old television drama, saying that she will be contacted by phone, don't call the police, and all that rubbish.

Then I get to the amount they are asking for, and I give a little cry. The paper shakes in my fingers.

He laughs. "Thought that two hundred and fifty thousand would get to you!"

He rubs the finger with the bandage on it. I hope it hurts like hell.

I have my mouth open to tell him he's crazy, that it won't work. Then I remember my weapon of silence, and I close my mouth again. It doesn't matter what I tell this man. He'll follow whatever plan he's made.

"Dammit," he says. "I wish you'd talk. You got to do everything the hard way?"

They'll send this letter, or one like it, no matter what I do. I don't think Cristabel will give them the money. She can't!

As though he could read my mind, he says, "You haven't got a choice. Sign it."

His laugh terrifies me more than his words. This man is out of his mind. So I sign, misspelling my name, putting an "e" where the "i" should be. It's the only thing I can think of to do.

He takes the paper from me, reads it, and seems satisfied. "Okay, girl," he says. "I'll bring you some food in a little while, before it gets dark. There won't be any light down here while it's dark. Don't want anything to look strange to the neighbors."

He leaves, clumping up the steps. The door shuts and locks.

So there are neighbors. Can something be done about attracting their attention? I'll have to think about it.

I feel exhausted now, drained. I look forward to sleep. There's a towel and soap in the bathroom at least, but I wish I had my hairbrush. There's one in my bag. I wonder if they brought my handbag with them. It was hanging over my shoulder, I think, when they took me. Did I drop it? I must have, and I can't remember.

He's following a plan. Did he make the plan? If he did, it must have holes in it. He's too dumb to make a really foolproof kidnapping plan. But maybe someone else made it.

I listen to the footsteps moving over my head. *Who are you?* I want to cry out. *What are you doing up there?* I shove the sleeve of my sweater into my mouth to keep from screaming. I must hang on! I've got to!

A little later I am wrapped in my blanket, leaning against the wall, breathing evenly, deeply. I try to make my trembling body relax. I start with my toes and work upward, concentrating on letting each muscle loosen. The calves of my legs are heavy, my mind croons in a soft pattern. They are heavy...growing heavy...my thighs are heavy...they are relaxing, relaxing...my legs are so heavy....

The click of the lock at the top of the stairs causes me to jump violently. My mental exercise has been wiped out. I wait tensely as the man comes down the stairs. He carries a tray. I smell food. Something at the back of my mind registers a remembrance of something. But what? I don't know. I lose the thought.

Without a word he comes to the table and

puts down the tray. His eyes are wary. They watch me carefully, and there is a strange, alert look in them.

"Here's something for you to eat," he says. "The way I promised."

There are two plates on the tray, and a glass of milk. Both plates are covered with inverted faded-green plastic bowls. He waits and watches. I hesitate, but there is no point in waiting. Apparently he wants to stay here while I eat. Then he'll take the tray and leave me alone until morning.

Shrugging back the blanket, I lean forward and remove the bowl from the nearest plate. I shriek and the bowl flies from my hand. On the plate is a bloody mouse!

For a moment I gag, my hands at my throat, my eyes riveted to the plate in spite of my revulsion. Then I realize that what I am looking at is a rubber mouse, and he has poured ketchup over it! Sick! Horrible! What a crazy, sick thing to do!

I am so furious that I jump to my feet and try to strike out at him. I try to rip that stupid ski mask from his head, to scratch, to hurt him.

"You bastard!" I scream at him. It's the worst thing I can think of to call this man.

But he laughs as he grabs my wrists and holds them tightly. "I knew I could get you to talk, girl! It wasn't even that hard!"

I struggle, and he says in a deeper, more intense voice, "Don't try to take off this mask. You're safe enough now, but if you can identify me, then I might have to kill you."

I'm so angry and scared that I begin to sob, and the tears flood my eyes. He becomes nothing but a blur.

"Now, look here, don't get so upset," he says. "I thought it was a good joke, myself. Hey, girl, don't cry like that."

But I can't stop. I shake with my sobs, and it's hard to stand up. I find I am leaning against him, completely unable to do what I want to do, which is to keep cool and stay as far away from this man as possible.

He murmurs things, trying to get me to stop crying, and I feel as though I were a small child and he were my father. I am dependent on him for my life. The thought robs me of whatever strength I have left.

Finally the sobs become dry. There are no tears left. He leads me back to the cot, and I sit on it, waiting to be told what to do.

"Eat your dinner now," he says. He takes away the plate with the toy mouse.

"I can't," I whisper. "How do I know what's under the other bowl?"

"Listen," he says, "be a good sport. I owed you one for that bowl of soup you threw at me. I owe you one for my sore finger, too; but if I decide to collect on that, it will come later."

He pulls off the plastic bowl and nods toward the tray. "See, it's a nice hamburger—just the way you'll like it."

And then I know.

That needle of remembrance pricks again, and the record falls into place.

The voice is the same. The way he said the word "hamburger." It's got to be Zack.

And is the one upstairs his wife...Loretta?

I can't let him know that I've guessed who he is. He said he might have to kill me if I identified him. I obediently reach for the hamburger, my hands shaking.

"You sure look a mess, you know that?" Zack says.

I don't answer. I take a small bite of the hamburger and chew it softly. It's delicious. How can I sit here and munch on a hamburger and think about how much I like it and be so scared at the same time? It's as if there were two of me.

"I'm not going to bother you," he says. "You just relax and enjoy your dinner. I'll come down in the morning to get the tray."

I look up at him, and he adds, "You hear me?"

"Yes," I whisper. "Thank you."

I don't pay much attention as he leaves. I am concentrating on my hamburger, trying to make it last. I finish it and drink the milk, and realize that the light is almost gone. I had better wash my face before it is too dark to see where I am going.

It takes only a few minutes, but darkness is racing me and I can barely find my cot as I come back from the bathroom.

I climb between the sheets, trying to straighten my blanket, being careful to tuck it in tightly around the edges, so that loose ends can't trail on the floor. I don't know what might come rustling out of the cracks. I have an instant of panic as I think of the large tree roaches and imagine I hear dozens of them scurrying around. But I force myself to push the thoughts away.

So many hours have passed since I last slept, and some of the effects of the drug they gave me must still be with me. I am ungodly tired. All I want to do is sleep. I don't even try to plan what to do next. I don't even wonder what will happen to me. I simply roll on one side, my back against the wall, smelling the musty dampness of the basement walls and the hot-iron fragrance of the sheets, the sour smell of the fear still in my throat.

When I get the blue eye shadow at the store, I'd better get some mouthwash. The incongruity of that random thought seems so hysterical that I find wild laughter rising in the back of my throat. "No!" I command myself. "Keep calm."

Steadily I push it back, push thoughts of any kind back into a void. Soon I am asleep.

[FOUR]

I DREAM THAT Zack is standing at the foot of my cot. He is standing quietly, his arms folded, staring at me. I wake with a cry, kicking out, revolted and terrified.

But no one is there.

Pale morning light filters through the dirty windows near the ceiling, illuminating the room. There is no one in this room but me.

My dream has told me something about myself. There is another reason for my fear. This man, Zack, has the power to do anything he wants to me, but my mind has been pushing this thought away. Now I analyze it. What will I do if he tries…

My mind won't complete the sentence. I

huddle on my cot, pulling the blanket around my shoulders, and shiver. I feel cruddy, and wish I could take a bath. Maybe it's better to look the way I must look. I would like to be as repulsive to Zack as he is to me.

I get up and walk around the room. I must have some exercise. I try to do a few of the standing exercises that are the delight of our gym teacher, and which I must have done over a million times since first-grade outdoor-activity period. It does help to clear my brain as I breathe harder, and I think I must remember to tell her that the exercises really do have some benefit—especially when one is kidnapped. I giggle irrationally.

It's hard to live in a basement by yourself and wonder how long you'll be there and what will happen to you. I make myself think of something else, fearful that I'll come close to panic if I begin to understand my situation. I'll go over my French verbs. No, I won't. I hate French verbs. I don't hate France, just its verbs. I would love to go to France with the girls in my class. But I can't. Why can't I? Rosella is going to Chicago. Big deal. I wish I weren't in school. I wish I had a job so that I could earn enough money to go to France with the junior class. But if I weren't in school, I wouldn't be in the junior class. Nothing makes sense. I'm hungry.

I hear footsteps over my head. The kitchen must be over the basement. Someone is going to make breakfast. If I were at home, we'd have a big breakfast before going to church. It's seven o'clock now, and my father always wakes us early. Eggs and sausages and... When my father isn't being pompous about his religion, he can unbend a little. There are times when we almost come close to loving each other. Almost.

Tears are running down my cheeks, and it surprises me. I didn't know I was crying. Why is it that part of my mind seems to stay very cool and part of it is going bonkers? Do people in prison feel like this? Maybe not. At least people in prison know where they are and what's going on. If I could know that, maybe I'd be all right.

I walk to the foot of the steps and peer upward at the solid, forbidding door. What if I could force it open? Last night I went to sleep like a little kid being put to bed. Why didn't I stay awake until the people upstairs had gone to bed, and then I could at least try the door and see if it were possible to break out. What's the matter with me?

Tonight, I promise myself. Tonight I'll do it. Maybe there is something around this basement I can use to work on the door lock. The basement is as clean as it could possibly get. It looks as though no one has ever used this room. Except for the massive heating unit at one side and the cot and table for me, there is nothing in this basement. I walk over to the furnace to examine it. There is a door in the side with a little latching kind of handle. I pull on the handle, and the latch lifts scratchily through the rust. I swing the door open and see a large, hollow drumlike cavern. I poke my head inside to look at it. The pipes lead into it, and a funny thing happens. I hear Zack talking to someone!

I pull my head out again, and the sound is muffled. Apparently these pipes lead from the heating unit to registers in the rooms. Some of the vents must be open, even though the heater isn't in use, and through those open vents the voices are carried and magnified in this hollow metal expanse.

Maybe I can find out what is happening. I need to know what they are going to do with me.

I put my head back inside the furnace and listen. Zack is still talking. I pity his wife.

"Don't tell me you're setting up that old ironing board again!" he says. "You ain't even got the breakfast dishes cleared, and you're fixing to iron. What for?"

"I want to iron," the voice comes back. "You know I like the sheets and dish towels and things ironed. It just makes me feel right." Is this voice Loretta's? She didn't talk to me, so I have no idea what she sounds like. This voice is high-pitched and slow-speaking, with a drawl. Sounds more like a Southerner than a Texan. I bet she's not very bright. She couldn't have her head together if she married Zack.

"That girl down there—take her the tray," the woman says. "The stuff on it's getting cold."

"Don't rush me," Zack says. "There's still a good slurp in this coffee cup."

I shut the furnace door carefully, so it won't make a sound. I go back to the cot and sit on it, waiting patiently.

The door at the top of the stairs opens, and I tense. I try to push away the thought of how frightened of this man I am. I don't want him to come near me; yet I need the food he's bringing, and I need him as a source of information.

He walks across the room, still wearing the ski mask, and puts the tray on the table. Then he stands at the foot of my cot, staring at me, looking as he did in my dream, his eyes pale reflections of my terror. I begin to tremble. I can't stop.

"Hey, girl, what's the matter with you?" Zack asks.

"I—I'm cold," I stammer.

"Well, just keep that blanket around you then," he says. "There's no way to get the chill out of this basement." He laughs heartily. "It's a really pretty, sunny day outside. Going to be nice and warm out there!"

I huddle inside myself, hating him for his cruelty. His voice changes, and there is a tone of sympathy in it. "Listen here, I was just kidding.

I don't like keeping you down here any more than you like being here."

My words burst out in a shout. "Then why are you doing this to me?"

Zack folds his arms across his chest. He is wearing a clean T-shirt today, thank goodness. It even looks ironed. Surely his wife doesn't iron his T-shirts, too?

He shrugs. "It's only business. Didn't you ever want to get into a good business proposition and maybe have to look the other way at some things you didn't like too much? No, I guess you didn't, being who you are."

He has told me more than he knows. He has essentially told me that someone else thought this up and he went in on the idea. It wasn't Loretta. That's for sure. So someone else planned this kidnapping. Who? Is there any way in the world I can get him to tell me the name?

I suppose not. He is keeping his own name from me—or so he thinks. It would be dangerous for me to know too much, and yet I've got to find out as much as I can without letting Zack realize he has given information away.

Trying to stay as cool as possible, I reach over and slide the tray closer to me. The coffee is bitter and cold. The eggs are jelled in their grease. The toast is hard. It doesn't matter. I'm hungry, so I begin to eat.

"Have you been in contact with my grandmother yet?" I ask Zack.

He grins under that stupid ski mask. "That's for me to know and you to find out," he says.

That's third-grade dumbness, I think, remembering the age at which we chanted that at each other every chance we got. Then it comes to me that third-grade mentality is probably where Zack stopped. How do you reach a third grader in an appeal to reason? How do you convince him that he shouldn't harm you, should let you go, should be fair?

We weren't very fair in the third grade. We weren't fair to each other at all. Things seem more hopeless than ever. I polish off the coffee and lean back against the wall. The coldness of the cement seeps through the blanket, my sweater, and my shirt. I shiver again.

He reaches over to take the tray, and I try again. "Please tell me if you've reached my grandmother or my parents. I need to know. What did they say?"

"I told you," he says smugly, "that's for me..."

I can't bear hearing that horrible phrase again. "Wait!" I interrupt him. I desperately try to reach through to his emotions. Maybe there is something about this man that will respond. I must find out what that is. "How would you feel if you were in my place?" I ask him. "Don't you know how frightened I am?"

"That's the way it goes," he says. "You ain't supposed to be enjoying yourself all shut up down here."

"It's like being in jail," I snap at him. "You'd know about that, wouldn't you?"

"Maybe," he says. He stands there, balancing the tray, his head slightly cocked to one side as he studies me. "You sure do look a mess, girl. Don't you want to fix yourself up?"

I can't keep my body from stiffening as he says this, and he laughs, aware of what I'm thinking, I guess. "Don't worry," he says. "I ain't fixing to touch you. You don't appeal to me."

What he says strikes him as terribly funny, and he laughs all the way up the stairs.

I breathe a long sigh of relief and pull the blanket around me more tightly. I want to go home.

It's important to keep my mind busy, I know, so I go over what Zack has said. He's told me three things without being aware of it. The first, that someone else planned this kidnapping. The second, that things are going the way they planned them, or he wouldn't be so cheerful. And the third, that he has already been in prison. This isn't the first time he's done something criminal.

Curious, I wonder what he was arrested for. He's the type I'd think could easily get into a fight with someone in a bar. Or rob one of those small, late-night grocery stores, wearing that stupid ski mask. Or maybe burgle apartment houses when the people in the apartments weren't home. Do you say "burgle"? It doesn't sound right. I have no idea what Zack could have done. For all I know, he was in prison for murder.

Murder?

That could be me, couldn't it? The panic begins to rise again from that spot at the pit of my stomach, and I think I'm going to be sick.

But the door opens suddenly, and I am startled, distracted.

Zack comes down the stairs carrying a hairbrush. He gives it to me with a shake of his head. "You really need this," he says.

I take it, wondering. It's my own hairbrush—the wooden brush with the natural bristles that I keep in the drawer of my own dressing table at home. Where did he get it? And what else of mine has he brought here?

"This is mine," I say stupidly, still holding out the hairbrush.

"I know it," he says.

"But how…?"

"Don't ask so many questions," he says, but he still sounds good-natured, pleased with himself.

"Just tell me this," I plead. "Do you have any of my other things? These clothes…"

He waves a hand. "I know. You'd like to clean up. Well, give us some time. We got it all worked out."

I take a step toward him. "Please, I need…"

"Listen, girl," he says sharply, and I stop where I am standing. "I wasn't supposed to bring you this, even. I just got tired of seeing you look the way you look. A rabbit running through a mud puddle looks cleaner than you do."

He turns and starts up the stairs. Quickly, surprising myself, I ask, "Could I have a book?"

"Huh? A book? What are you talking about?"

"I would like a book," I tell him. "I need something to keep my mind occupied. Otherwise, I'll go crazy down here. Couldn't you please let me have a book to read?"

"Where do you think I'm going to get a book?"

"Why...surely you must have some books in your house."

He thinks a minute. "I'm not one for reading, but my...Well, I'll look around and see what I can find."

"Thank you," I say. "Thank you very much."

He chuckles. "I'm a pretty nice kind of guy," he says. "You gotta admit I take good care of you down here."

I nod.

"Say it," he tells me.

"You do. You take good care of me." Who is

saying these words? This is part of a crazy nightmare.

He laughs again and goes up the stairs. I hear the click as the door locks.

I am wary of this man. He is kind only when it amuses him to be kind. If anything should go wrong, I am afraid he would hurt me with no more thought or emotion than he gave to my request for a book. I don't know how to protect myself. Sometimes I feel totally dependent on him, and I don't like the feeling. I don't know what to do.

The water runs until it is hot, and I scrub my face and arms, then rub them briskly with the rough towel. It's cold, so I put my sweater back on, and I start on the tangles in my hair, brushing it so hard my scalp tingles and my eyes water. But soon the hairbrush slides in smooth strokes down my long hair, and it feels much better. I wish there were a mirror in this bathroom. I wish there were a tub, so I could take a bath. I want so badly to go home.

I turn, flipping the hair back from my face, and see Zack standing there, watching me. Before I can stop myself, I gasp. I quickly step out of the bathroom, embarrassed to be there with a man watching me.

Zack tosses a book on the bed. "It's the only thing I could find. She likes to read these books, but she takes them back to the paperback bookstore and trades them when she's finished them. This one she hadn't got to return yet."

"Who's 'she'?"

He doesn't answer my question. He says, "You look a lot better now with your hair combed and your face washed. Think I'll just let you keep the hairbrush. You'll need it."

"Thank you," I say.

He turns, and I add, "And thank you for the book."

He looks back at me when he reaches the stairs. "You sure are a funny girl with your 'thank you's and all those manners. I sure as hell wouldn't say 'thank you' to anyone who did me the way I did you."

I have no answer, so I just watch him as he goes up the stairs and locks the door again. He's right. Why should I say "thank you" to him for anything? Do these polite responses go so deeply that they mean nothing in the long run? I must remember to tell Madame DeJon. Instead of teaching us to be so damned polite, she could add a self-defense class to the curriculum. Kicking, stomping, gouging—I wish I knew how they were done. If I ever get out of here, I'm going to learn how and...if ever...

Fight down the panic. Switch to a new thought. Think positive. Where's that book?

I pick up the paperback and look at the cover. A girl, in what looks like a filmy nightgown, is running down a hill from a spooky-looking castle—just like all those Gothic mysteries Lorna reads. They all seem to have the same cover—just different girls and different castles. Well, now I'll find out what a Gothic is like. Lorna would be pleased. She's always trying to get me to read hers.

I settle myself on the cot with the book and my hairbrush. I keep the hairbrush on my lap as I would a security blanket. It's my link with home. I busy myself reading until I get to the heroine's second run-in with the brooding man with dark, curly hair. I think if I read "his tanned, muscular arms" one more time I'll get sick and throw the book across the room. I look at my watch. Time is going so slowly.

Outside, there are the faint voices of children playing. I wish they would come closer. Maybe I could make them hear me. But they are shouting in their play, and they must be quite a distance away. No one would hear me yelling except Zack, and I can't afford to make him angry.

The footsteps are over my head again. When they were talking earlier, they were in the kitchen, from what Zack said about finishing his coffee. Maybe I can listen in again. I might learn something.

The door to the furnace scratches and squeaks a little as I open it. My hands are damp with nervous sweat. Keep cool. They can't hear this small noise up in the kitchen.

I lean over and put my head inside the empty drum. The voices have a metallic, echoing sound. I can hear the clink of spoons and pots. Loretta—or whoever she is—must be cooking something for lunch.

If there is a third person involved in all this, where is he? Has he come to the house? Does Zack meet him somewhere else?

"How long is it going to take you to fix that spaghetti?" Zack asks.

"I'm working on it," the woman says.

"You sure are a slow one, Loretta," he says.

I nod, as though ticking off another fact. It is the woman I met. It is Loretta. And I can identify both Zack and Loretta to the police when I'm out of this place.

There is a long pause while Loretta is busy doing something up there. The kitchen noises are familiar sounds in this unreal world I'm in. I feel the way I did when I was a little kid lying on the sofa and recuperating from the mumps or flu or something and hearing someone in the kitchen making me a custard or a bowl of soup. It's a false sense of security, but the feeling comes over me, and I remind myself that I am standing in a damp basement with my head inside an unused heating unit, listening to the people who have imprisoned me here. The total thought doesn't come into focus, but it's just as well. If it did, I might start screaming.

I hear Loretta say, "Zack, I'm nervous about this whole thing. We're going to get caught."

"We're too smart to get caught," he says. His voice is smugly self-satisfied.

I keep thinking I've heard this dialogue in an old Humphrey Bogart movie. Do movies really happen to people? Is that why I'm here?

Zack goes on bragging. "The way this thing is set up, there is no way we can go to jail, even if we do get caught."

"Are you sure?"

"I'm positive. It's the most foolproof thing I was ever in on."

She grunts. "You were never in on anything good. Show me what you ever got from one of those schemes you got talked into."

There is the sound of a chair slamming down. He must have tipped it up, resting his feet on the table. I picture him standing up, getting angry with his wife. But the tone of his voice surprises me. There is a sense of delight and accomplishment in it.

"Listen, Loretta," he says, "I know I've given you a hard time, but this is different. When we get away from here with our share of the money, you'll see. You'll like South America. We'll get us all the good things we never had before. I promise."

"But what if we get caught?" she repeats. I notice that her voice has a constant whine in it, a twangy sound, like a loose guitar string.

"Nothing to worry about," he says. "We'll be back where we started, but that's the worst that can happen to us."

"You're sure?"

"It's all set up. I told you that."

"There ain't been a thing in the papers or on radio and TV about the kidnapping. It's creepy, like it never happened."

"The grandma's just using good sense," he says. He laughs. "Just doing what she was told to do. Now, quit worrying, 'cause I'm getting sick of it."

She gives a long sigh. "Open that jar of spaghetti sauce. Do you want to take the girl her lunch or eat yours first?"

Apparently Loretta, too, is used to doing what she is told.

I don't wait to hear the answer. I certainly don't want to get caught listening in here. Carefully, I close the door and walk back to the cot. I pick up the book and begin to read at the place where I left off.

"He lifted her in his tanned, muscular

arms…" I wince, clench my teeth, and plod through.

Later I'm going to see if I can pull the hinge from the door of the furnace. Maybe I can use it to work the lock free on the door that is keeping me here. All I can do is try. The thought gives me something to hang on to.

[FIVE]

THE DAY goes so slowly. I finish the Gothic. Funny, as I turn the last page and close the book, I can't remember what the story was about. I sit on my cot, staring at the cover. Why did the woman in the story run outside in her nightgown? As a matter of fact, I don't think she really ever ran anywhere in her nightgown. Shouldn't the picture on the cover have something to do with the story?

Zack only comes to the basement once, and that is to bring me a makeshift evening meal of chili and crackers. The chili reeks of onions and grease. He says something about a television show he wants to watch, and I realize today must be Sunday. I am getting mixed up about the days, even though I haven't been here that long.

The latch on the furnace is loose. The screw that held it was stiff in my fingers at first, but after a few taps with the heel of my shoe, it began to loosen and turn fairly easily. I am afraid to remove it until tonight. Zack seems to notice everything.

Now that I've decided to try to escape, I can talk to Zack without that horrible helpless feeling that I am living just on his whim. I ask him about my grandmother, but he doesn't answer me. He still seems to be in good spirits. That's in my favor. I have to wait until they are asleep to try to open the door. But I am going to try.

I sit with my legs tucked under me, in case there are any roaches scurrying across the cold cement. It's almost too dark to see anything, but by this time I know the floor plan of this room so well I am sure I'll be able to find my way around. I don't know why I'm so tired, so sleepy. I've tried to keep up my exercises. Once, in psychology class, Miss Dobbins mentioned that sleep can be an escape mechanism. Maybe I am trying to escape that way, because it's terribly hard for me to keep my eyes open. The musty, damp smell has crept over the room again. Outside my window I can hear crickets chirping in the tangled grass and, far off, traffic, as though we are near a busy freeway.

There seem to be tiny rustlings and whisperings around me, and I try to force them from my mind so that my imagination won't inflate them into horrors that could end in a scream. I think about my family...about my mother.

For the first time I see what my mother really looks like. I have looked at her all my life, and it surprises me that she has always been just a face and body that I take for granted, perpetually old. Why have I always thought of my mother as an old woman? Do all children think that? But as I scan my mental image of her face, I see an attractive, middle-aged woman. Her hair, which is a light brown, not dark like mine, hangs free in a perfect cut. Her makeup covers flawless skin, which seems to glow. Maybe the bottles and jars on her dressing table are responsible for that naturally healthy look. Even her false eyelashes look real.

As I look into her eyes, I see a faint sadness there. She always seems cheerful. Is there something in my mother's life that isn't what it appears to be on the surface? I shake my head, wondering at my obtuseness. Of course. There has to be. No one is the same inside as on the surface.

My father met my mother in college. Her family was comfortably middle class, living somewhere in Iowa. We went to visit my grandmother—my mother's mother—a few years before she died. I remember overhearing her say that my mother had made a good marriage. I guess that meant she had married into the Cristabel Lattimore money. I don't think of money as making a good marriage. I think a good marriage is one in which I am terribly in love with someone, and he's just as much in love with me.

I wonder how my mother felt when she got married. Did she feel proud of herself for being a beautiful woman in love, or did she tiptoe into marriage with the Lattimore name and money, hoping she'd be worthy of the position? As I look deeply into her eyes, I think I can see how she felt, and tears burn my eyelids.

My poor, poor mother. You are still afraid of them, aren't you? You expend all your energies trying to please them. A rush of love and pity chokes me. I want to tell my mother that I understand her and that I really do love her, but she isn't here.

I wipe my eyes on the blanket and gulp away the tears. It is quiet upstairs. It has been quiet for some time now. Are Zack and Loretta asleep, or are they in another room, watching television? I have no way of knowing. I have no way of finding out the time, either, since I can't see my watch. It could be eight o'clock or it could be midnight. Existence in a black hole has no time.

But I'm impatient. I've got to do something or go bananas. So I get up from the cot, try not to think of roaches, and move slowly to the furnace, arms outstretched. When I touch it, the metal is cold, and I jump involuntarily. It's a weird feeling, touching something cold and unseen in a dark place. My fingers find the door, however, and I feel for the latch. It is quite rusty, and as I wiggle it again, it seems even looser than it was before. It's hard to tell. When I could see it, I could keep it in perspective. Without the sense of sight here in the pitch-darkness, even the size and shape of the latch seem over-large and clumsy.

The latch fits through a groove, with a single screw holding it in place. I work the screw with my fingers, and it loosens. I am able to turn it. But it comes out too quickly, and the screw drops to the floor, the latch with it. The sound seems exaggerated—a clank that could be heard all over the house. I hold my breath and wait, but nothing happens. I exhale slowly.

I have let my fear take over again. Carefully I get down on my hands and knees and feel over the floor until my fingers touch the latch. I grip it, scramble to my feet, and move toward the stairs.

I misjudge my distance and bang my toes on the bottom step. What if Zack heard that? What if he is waiting just behind the door, at the top of the stairs? The door opens inward, into the kitchen, I suppose. Will I work and work on the lock, only to open the door and see Zack there, grinning at me?

The thought so unnerves me that I can't move from my spot at the bottom of the stairs.

I can only stare up into the darkness where the door should be, thinking of that sneering grin. My hands shake, and I almost drop the latch again.

As I grab for it, the spell is broken, and I am able to function. I grope for the rough boards, which make a kind of railing, and take a step upward. The railing quivers, and I realize that it wouldn't support my weight if I should fall. I'll have to be very, very careful.

One slow step at a time I climb the stairs, occasionally stubbing a toe, since they are rough cement steps, unequal in size. It occurs to me with a burst of excitement that if there were someone in the room on the other side of the door, light would show through the cracks. It is dark. Zack and Loretta must be asleep. They have to be!

I reach the door. It's hard and cold under my hands. I find the doorknob, but what can I do now? I try to slip the rusty metal latch into the door frame where the lock enters, but it is too thick. The hinges are on the other side of the door, or I could work on separating those. The only thing I can think of doing is to try to dig away the wood around the lock. The wood must be old, and on the basement side, where it is constantly slightly damp, it might be rotten enough to give.

I dig at the door frame with all my strength, trying to gouge out the splinters of wood. But God knows how many coats of paint have protected this wood. It's as hard as metal, and my chipping knocks away some flakes of paint, which flick at my fingers as they fall, but that's all. Finally, sweaty and out of breath, I admit to myself that there is no way I can get out of this place.

I drop the latch into the pocket of my sweater. I feel my way down the stairs and across to my cot. I know why people die of hopelessness. It comes on like a thick blanket, smothering your thoughts, your confidence, creeping into your mind and filling the corners. I lie in the dark, suffocating under horrible despair, wishing I were dead. I sleep, then wake, then sleep. The sleep is filled with monstrous dreams that attack, cry out, and vanish, leaving me once more awake and staring into the darkness. Help me! My mind is screaming, but there is no one to hear.

Morning comes. I have forgotten to wind

my watch, and it has stopped, so now I have no idea how late it is. I think I hear the voices of children again. Maybe they are going to school. Is this a school day? What day is it? I am totally disoriented. I can hear the children. If I scream and scream, will they hear me?

I pull my cot to the far wall and stand on it, trying to reach the window. At the top of my lungs I yell, "Help! Help!" Even stretching as far as I can, there is no way I can reach those nailed-shut, dirt-caked windowpanes. But I can't stop screaming and shouting, and I beat my hands against the rough walls until they hurt.

The door opens and Zack hurries down the stairs. "Cut that out!" he orders.

On command the noise stops, although it seems to be going on inside my head.

"Get off that thing," Zack says, and I climb down.

A part of me is behaving like an automaton, and another part is asking why I'm doing so.

I turn toward the cot, but he grabs my arm roughly, swinging me around. I raise a hand to protect myself, and it brushes against the rough wool of the ski mask. I begin to shudder uncontrollably until Zack shakes me so hard I cry out.

"What are you doing?" I manage to gasp.

"Trying to get you to calm down, girl," he says. He reaches up to adjust the mask, and his eyes seem faded into their sockets.

"I'm all right," I make myself say. I don't want him to shake me again.

"Go on up the stairs," he tells me. "And act like you got some brains. Don't try running off again."

I am too weak-kneed to run, but I hope he doesn't know that. My legs tremble as I climb the stairs. I am filled with relief that I am finally able to leave that horrible basement room, and at the same time I'm scared to death of what is going to happen next.

He follows me so closely that his breath is hot against my right shoulder, and it reeks of onions and stale beer. As we reach the door, I automatically stop as though I were programmed, but he pushes me roughly and says, "Go on through. Go ahead."

I step into a large kitchen. The room has the high ceiling of an old house, and the cupboards have been painted a nauseating shade of tan. Someone has applied red-rooster decals in the middle of each cabinet, and it strikes me that they are slightly crooked and off center. The linoleum is in an imitation brick pattern, also tan, and faded and worn toward the center of the kitchen. At one side is an ironing board with a steam iron resting on end.

"Get yourself a drink of water," Zack says. He stands there, watching me.

"I don't need a drink of water," I tell him.

His answer is to push me, and I catch my balance against the cabinets. "Open the cabinet over there," he says, pointing. "There's glasses inside. Get yourself a drink of water."

I can't figure out what he has in his mind. He acts like a person carrying out a plan. How could my having a drink of water carry out any kind of plan? If he were to hand me a glass of anything, the way he is acting, I would be suspicious and wouldn't want to drink it.

Obediently, I take a glass, turn on the faucet, and fill the glass to the brim. I begin to sip it.

"That's enough," Zack says. "Pour out the water and put the glass on the sink."

I do as he tells me, but I am more puzzled than I was before.

We move, at his direction, into a dining room, and I hear someone scuttling through the kitchen and down into the basement, making little mouse movements and trying to be as silent as possible. Could it be Loretta?

My mind is tired. That is the only word for it. I have gone through fear and anger and terror and exhaustion, and now I am blank, wondering what we are doing. I can't gather my thoughts together enough to put the pieces of this insane puzzle in place. Why would a kidnapper follow his victim from room to room in a house, telling her to pick up objects and put them down? The question floats without an anchor. I have no way of trying to answer it. I simply do as I am told.

We walk up the stairs with their old-fashioned machine-carved moldings that match the patterns in the moldings around the ceilings. I touch a wall switch, at Zack's direction, and low-watt bulbs in a multi-globed chandelier flicker on, lighting fat, full-blown, hand-painted roses from another era. I note that there is no dust, that everything is clean, even the faded brown carpet on the stairway.

At the door of the first room on the right, Zack tells me to stop. "Go inside," he says.

I open the door and walk into the room. At first I notice the yellowed imitation maple dresser and headboard and the flowered chenille bedspread with some of its fringe missing. But what catches my eye, and takes a moment to register, is my handbag on the dresser. Some of my things have spilled out of it—my lipstick, my comb, my toning lotion that is supposed to take care of acne and doesn't... but that wasn't in my handbag!

I turn to question Zack, my mind beginning to clear, but he pushes me again and again, with little nudges, until I catch myself, palms down on the dresser top for support.

"This is your stuff," he says. "And some of your clothes are in the closet."

"How did you get them?"

He laughs.

"How could you get my things out of my house?" I repeat the question.

"There are a couple of things I want you to do, girl," he says. He nods toward the far door to the room. It's open and leads to a bathroom.

I can see the white tile floor and the end of an old-fashioned claw-foot tub.

"You get in there and take a bath and wash your hair and fix yourself up."

"No," I say.

"Listen, your parents aren't going to want to see you looking like such a slob." His lips stretch in a grin behind that horrible mask.

It's hard to talk, to breathe, to think, but I manage to gasp, "I'm going home?"

"Sure," he says. "Told you there was nothing to worry about. Now, you just take off those dirty things you've got on, and put them in a pile here on the floor."

Instinctively I back away from him, and he shakes his head. "You been watching too many movies, girl. I won't be here. I've got things to do. There's a woman who'll be up here, keeping an eye on you." Sternly he adds, "And don't think about giving her any trouble, because she'll have a gun. I've told her to use it if she needs to."

I don't answer. There are too many thoughts in my head to get them sorted out into words. After a long silence his tone of voice becomes wheedling. "Look, now, just play along and don't think about making trouble, and you'll be home before you know it. If you start acting up, then somebody's going to get hurt, and that somebody is you."

I find myself nodding. What he says seems to make sense. I just want to go home. That's all I want. I can't trust this man. I know that. But there are few choices, and something tells me that the best thing I can do right now is follow the rules he's set up.

I see that my suitcase is on a spindly wooden chair over at the side of the room near the closet door. Zack walks out into the hall. There are some rustling movements, some whispers, and a woman comes into the room.

She stands watching me a moment. She is wearing a ski mask, identical with the one Zack was wearing. It seems incongruous with the rest of her clothing—her wide-bottomed jeans, the pink T-shirt that clings around the pudgy bulges where her midriff should be. It's Loretta. There is no doubt about it. Her eyes are small and wary. There is a gun in her hand.

She shuts the door to the hall behind her

and perches on the edge of the bed as though it were a stove heating up. Her gun hand looks awfully nervous.

"Do what he told you." It's the first time she's spoken to me. It's the same voice I heard echoed through the heat register into the basement.

"Okay," I tell her. I go into the bathroom and turn on the faucets. There's a brown stain from years of water dripping in a path down to the drain, but the tub is clean. Everything in this house is clean.

"Don't shut the door!" Her voice is strident, a little scared. She doesn't like this any more than I do. I'm glad she doesn't follow me into the bathroom. I'd hate to have her squeezed in here with her jittery gun while I'm trying to take a bath.

I drop my clothes on the floor, but she calls out, "Throw those things out here!" so I do, tossing them practically at her feet. Then I put my watch on the basin. I hurry into the tub and turn off the water. It's almost at the top of the tub, and in spite of my emotional state, I still delight in the warmth around my body. These old tubs are so deep. I decide I like them better than newer bathtubs. My bottle of shampoo is propped on the soap dish that hangs over the edge of the tub. They haven't forgotten a thing.

As I soap my hair and rub my scalp vigorously, I seem to get my thoughts back into focus. The warmth, the steam, the stinging of shampoo against my squeezed-together eyelids—it helps thoughts fall back into place.

I submerge, liking the sensation, holding my breath and rubbing shampoo from my hair while I'm underwater. When I spring up to a sitting position, I can think more clearly. My hair is dripping rivulets down my neck and shoulders.

I cap the shampoo and reach for the bar of soap. It feels so wonderful to be clean again. I would like to stay in the tub all day.

Loretta's voice snaps me back to reality. "You been in there long enough," she says. "Get out now and get dried. I got your clothes laid out on the bed for you."

There are two towels hanging against the wall, both of them smelling of irons and ironing boards. I'd never want to iron towels, and I don't think anyone could make Della do it, but

I have to admit that ironed towels smell awfully good and extra clean. I wrap my hair in one and dry myself with the other. I am beginning to feel renewed. I'm hungry. I might be ready to tackle Loretta, but there she sits with the gun in her hand, and it's pointed right at me.

"Put your clothes on, quick," she says.

I drop the towel and put on my bra and bikini panties. My gray slacks and red pullover shirt are on the bed. I know they were hanging in the closet the day I was kidnapped. I'm positive! Or am I? I've looked at my clothes and worn my clothes, but how can I be sure when I saw them last? When did these kidnappers get them? I must know the answer.

I straighten the shirt, pulling it over my hips, and reach up to towel-dry my hair. I wonder what happened to the clothes I tossed in here on the floor.

Loretta has moved from the bed to stand against the wall, and she waves the gun in my direction. "Sit down on the bed to do that," she says. "I don't want you to try anything funny. I really can shoot this here gun." She hands me my wristwatch.

My tongue is forming the name, but I catch

myself in time, breathing quickly as I realize I almost gave myself away. "He—the man who was here..." I say. "He said I would be going home."

"That's right," she says.

"I left my brush in the basement," I tell her. "Can I get it? I need to brush my hair."

"It's right here," she answers. She takes the hairbrush from the dresser and tosses it into my lap.

I watch her as I brush my hair. "Where did you get my clothes?"

"It doesn't matter."

"It does to me. Was it you who put the tape on the door? Did you steal them then?"

The gun wavers in her fingers. "Don't ask so many questions," she says. "Put on some lipstick, some makeup, whatever you're used to wearing."

I don't budge. "Why?"

She leans toward me as tense as the spring that holds our garage door. "Because I said so. I don't like this any more than you do, and I'm nervous as a cat having kittens, and I'm scared I might get riled enough to shoot you if you don't do what I tell you to do! You got that?"

"Yes," I say. "I understand." I fish through the things on the dresser and find what I need. In a few minutes I look healthy and normal, but I feel like Alice in Wonderland down the wrong hole, wondering what she's doing in a place like this. I know one thing for sure. I am not going to tangle with Loretta. She strikes me as being one step this side of a nervous breakdown.

I stand up and stare at her. Her eyes are bright gleams that remind me of the tiny lights that wink on and off on Christmas trees. She looks ready to short out. "What do you want me to do now?" I ask her, trying to keep my voice calm.

She waves the gun toward the door. Dear God, I hope it doesn't go off!

"Downstairs," she says. "Get yourself to that room in back—the one with the TV in it."

I walk down the stairs steadily. I've got my bearings now, thanks to that hot bath and shampoo. I try to get glimpses of the front street as we come into the small entry hall. It's an old neighborhood, and not too tidy. Across the street there is a junk car propped up on blocks and missing its wheels. A worn-out water heater lies with some miscellaneous trash by the driveway of the house next to it.

"Don't go craning your neck to see things," Loretta snaps. "It won't make you no never mind later. Just do what I told you to do."

"How do I get to the room in back?" I ask her. "I forget."

"Just turn left and go down the hall a ways. You'll come right to it." She doesn't need to remind me, but she does. "And I'm coming right after you with this gun."

I enter the room. It has the usual over-stuffed furniture and odd tables that came from another, out-of-fashion generation. In the corner, its glass like a blank face, is the television set. In front of it is a deep wing chair in a scratchy, wine-colored plush fabric.

"You turn on the TV," Loretta says, "and then sit in that chair and watch it."

"Watch television?" I am trying to figure out the reason for this.

"Do it!" Her voice is like a screech. She is making me terribly nervous. I wish she didn't have that gun.

Quickly I turn the television on, not caring what channel it's turned to.

The voices come on first, shouting and screaming in some television game, and I adjust the volume to low. The last thing in the world I want to hear right now is some middle-aged woman hysterically kissing an emcee because she's just won a year's supply of drain cleaner.

"Sit down now!" Loretta says.

I do, and I can feel the lumpy springs in the seat cushion. Who ever heard of springs in a seat cushion? No wonder they went out of style.

"Where are you?" I ask. The wings on the chair block out my vision.

"Right behind you," she answers.

"I wish you were sitting where I could see you."

"I got no intention of doing so."

"But it makes me nervous having you back there where I can't see what's happening."

"Just having you here in this house makes me nervous!" she says. "Shut up and watch that TV show."

"I don't even know what show it is." The remark sounds inane, but surprisingly she picks up on it.

"It's a pretty good one. Those people have to match the celebrities and get them all right or they don't win."

Cautiously, trying to keep her new mood, I say, "Do most of them lose?"

"Sure, but sometimes they win, and then they get cars and trips and all that stuff."

"Did you ever want to be on one of those shows?"

"Yeah," she says. "But there's no way we're going to get out to California, and you got to be there to get picked. Did you ever notice that the people they pick are..."

Her voice breaks and stops. Only the raucous noise from the set infiltrates the room. Then she screams the words, "Don't talk to me! Don't try nothing with me! He said I got to shoot you if you try anything!"

"I won't! I promise!" My answer tumbles out, and I grip the arms of the chair for support. This woman is really near the brink. I had better be very careful not to upset her.

I think about this a moment. Zack had been in good spirits. The idea of kidnapping someone hadn't seemed to bother him. But Loretta is frightened. He must be used to committing crimes. However, this might be the first time she's been involved with him in any kind of crime. The whole idea terrifies her. I heard her telling Zack she was afraid they'd be caught. Has she been lying awake at night wondering what would happen if they *were* caught? He told her it was foolproof, but she doesn't believe it. She doesn't trust him. Why? I wish I knew.

I would like to ask Loretta who else is involved. That husband of hers is too dumb to work out a complex scheme. There has to be a third person. I know there is. But I can't talk to Loretta. Not now.

There is a noise at the front door, and Loretta lets out a little scream. I instinctively duck, tucking my head on my knees, wrapping my arms around my head. "Don't shoot me!" I gasp. I think I say it aloud.

But a voice comes from the hallway. "It's me!" Zack shouts jubilantly. "We did it! We did it!"

"You got the money?" she cries.

"You bet I did. It all worked out the way it was planned."

"But you got back too soon. How did…?" There is a pause; then Loretta's voice comes out higher pitched, scared. "You didn't go to the airport and leave the car and take a taxi home in case you were followed?"

"I didn't need to do all that." Zack is bragging. "There was no one there but me when I picked up the money. That old lady paid attention. She didn't call in the cops."

"But you were supposed to…"

"Shut up," he says. "I'm feeling good, and I don't want you to nag me out of it. We got the money! That's what counts!"

I listen intently, my body ice-cold. Now what happens? What will they do to me?

I hear his voice close behind me. "Dont turn around, girl," he says, and I shiver. "You just stay where you are. Lean back in that chair and keep on watching TV. You do that, and nothing bad is going to happen to you."

There is no choice. I respond to what he has said, gripping the arms of the chair as though they were all I could cling to.

They move to the back of the room. I wonder if Loretta still has the gun in her hand. Part of my mind is clinging to the idea of escaping, but another, calmer part tells me to sit still, to do what they tell me, and soon I will be released. I really don't think they want to kill me. I hope I'm right. I clutch the arms of the chair.

Zack is talking in a low voice to Loretta, but I can hear bits of what he is saying. "There we are—the money is divided in half, and one of the halves is ours!"

I'm right! There *is* someone else involved! Will he come here for his share? Will I find out who he is?

"I want to go with you, not by myself!" Loretta's voice is a wail of fear.

He shushes her, and I can't hear what they are saying. This damn television program! Even with the volume turned low, the maniac contestants and the emcee seem to be having a contest to see who can scream the loudest.

My breathing is shallow. I am straining hard to hear Zack and Loretta, to find out anything and everything I can so that I can tell the police when I'm safe again. I'm determined that these people will be caught and that my grandmother will get her money back!

I am living in a little ball of a world, ears tuned to the far wall behind me, eyes closed, trying to shut out any part of the intruding quiz show, nothing real to me except the lumpy springs in the chair and the rough plush upholstery that is scratching my arms and back. Then the world explodes around me.

There is a smashing noise at the front door! Voices are shouting! Footsteps bang down the hallway. My heart is banging, too. There is a blackness of terror that is blotting out my vision. I hear Loretta scream, and it pulls me together.

"Police!" someone is shouting in a deep voice.

"Take this!" Loretta yells in my ear. There is a thump as the gun lands in my lap.

Instinctively I clutch it and stand, hanging on to the chair back. Loretta and Zack are not wearing ski masks. They are standing at the door, hands in the air. They are backing into the room. It's all unreal in a speeded-up film. I am terrified at the quick motion, the noise. What's happening?

Three uniformed policemen burst through the doorway. One of them waves a warrant. The other two push Zack and Loretta against the nearest wall and begin searching them.

One of them yells at me, "Drop it!"

I can only stare at him. My mouth opens, but nothing comes out.

"I said drop that gun! Now!" His voice is hard. He means business.

I realize for the first time that I still have Loretta's gun in my hand.

I want to tell the man who I am, what I am doing here, but I can only stare at the gun he is holding—the one he is pointing at me!

[SIX]

I FIND MY voice. "What if it goes off?" I squeak. For some insane reason I think about an English teacher's remark that guns dropped on floors in all those TV police shows should by rights go off and hit someone.

A tall, muscular man in a beige checked sports coat the color of his hair enters the room. He doesn't look panicky. He looks at me reassuringly.

"Christina Lattimore?" he asks.

"Yes."

He walks toward me, holding up his badge. "Give me the gun, please," he says, and in one smooth motion reaches out for it. I put it into his hand. He looks at it, checks the safety, and tucks it into his belt.

"It's not my gun," I tell him, but he holds up a hand to silence me.

"I'd rather you didn't say anything until I read you your rights."

"But I..."

A look from him silences me. "All of you," he says, his gaze seeming to bore into Zack and Loretta, "pay attention. I'm Detective Jason York, and I'm going to read your rights to you." He takes a small, blue, plastic-covered card from his wallet and reads, "I want to advise you that you have the right to remain silent. Anything you say can and will be used against you in a court of law. You have the right to consult with a lawyer and..."

My mind turns off. I hear the words, yet at the same time I'm not hearing them. What is he doing? I'm the one who was kidnapped. Does he think I'm one of the criminals just because I was holding the gun Loretta threw in my lap? I don't understand what this is all about! He called me by name. Surely he knows I'm the victim here! He must know!

He has finished reading and is tucking the

card back into his wallet. In the quick moment of silence I say, "What are you doing? I'm Christina Lattimore. These people kidnapped me!"

Zack has not looked at me, but now he whirls, his eyes wide and scared. The policeman next to him grabs his arm.

"I'm not taking the blame for a kidnapping!" Zack yells. "She worked this thing out to look like a kidnapping! She wanted to get the money from her grandmother! You saw her holding the gun!"

They are all staring at me, and I feel as though I were out of my body, standing aside and looking at a play someone wrote, something I know can't be real. Loretta glances at the money, still in two piles on the table, and begins to cry.

"I knew we'd get caught!" Loretta wails.

"Wait!" I gasp. "Please, listen to me! This isn't true! That man is lying!"

"Do you know these people?" Detective York asks me.

"Yes," I say. Then I realize how bad that sounds, and stumble over the words in my fright. "They work at a hamburger stand beside the Katy freeway, and I go there, and…That is, the man does. His name is Zack, and I met his wife on Friday, when she came over to my table to talk to me."

"What did she talk about?"

"Well, nothing. She really didn't say a word. I mean…I know it doesn't sound right, but that's the way it is. You have to believe me."

Loretta breaks in. "I didn't want any part of this! She talked Zack into it, and I had to go along! It's not right for her to get out of it now!"

"I don't believe this! It's not true!" I hear myself shouting, but I begin to cry so hard I can't talk. Someone takes me by the shoulders and leads me to a chair. He keeps his hands on my shoulders, and his firm grip is reassuring. The sobs turn into snuffles and hiccups and sighs. I'm glad when I find a tissue in my hand. Through it all I hear someone else come in and say, "Those damn TV crews have just poured out on the front lawn."

One of the policeman asks, "Is that guy from New York there? That one with the glasses?"

"Yeah," the man says. "He's sure been a pain in the butt." He clears his throat.

"I've seen him around your division," the policeman says. "Told my wife about him. You know he talks all the time just the way he talks on TV? Sure is funny, hearing anybody talk like that."

Detective York comes around to squat in front of my chair, and an older man with a mustache moves to stand beside him. His jacket reeks of cigarette smoke, and there is a large brown stain on two fingers of his right hand.

"This is my partner, Detective Bill Waller," Detective York says.

I find myself saying, "I'm pleased to meet you," while a hysterical voice inside my head is asking, "Do you have to be so stupidly polite under any circumstances?"

"Apparently we've got a few things to sort out here," Detective York tells me. "I think we might talk about it now, before we go downtown."

"I want to go home," I tell him. "I want my mother and father to know I'm all right."

"They know," he says. "Bill got in touch with someone downtown, who'll contact them."

"I want to go home," I repeat, sounding as though I were only five years old.

"Let's talk a moment," he says. "We've got two conflicting stories we need to discuss—especially since we found you with a gun in your hand."

I tense, but he touches my arm. "Calm down," he says. "No one's going to interrupt you. Just take a deep breath and tell us what happened."

So I start at the beginning, with seeing someone in front of me with a ski mask over her head. I know now that it was Loretta. I tell him about the basement and how Zack took me upstairs so I could clean up. Its hard to talk about. Sometimes my voice breaks, and sometimes Zack yells out something, but Detective York stops him.

Finally, I lean back in my chair and let out a long, shuddering breath. "And that's all, I guess."

"You've told us all you can remember?"

"I may remember something later. I don't know."

He stands up. "We'll have to ask for your story again when we get downtown."

"Then why did I have to tell you now?"

"Because we're at the scene here. There

may be something you've said that we can check out quickly—something important."

Zack speaks up now. "I can tell you something!" he says. "That part about her staying in the basement! She's crazy! There's nothing like that down in the basement. We got a cot, but it's in a closet someplace. Go check it out, if you don't believe me."

Jason York nods toward one of the policemen in the doorway, and the man leaves. I am surprised to notice how many policemen are in the room. Why do they all need to be here?

"You said they both wore ski masks," he tells me.

"That's right. They look alike. They're black with a red stripe around the bottom."

Zack laughs at this, but it's a humorless laugh—one with cruelty in it. "Sure, I have a ski mask," he says. "But I've just the one. It's an old thing with some gloves to match. I used to wear it when I rode my motorcycle during cold weather. Haven't done that for a long time."

"Where is it?" Detective Waller asks him.

"I dunno," Zack says. He turns to Loretta. "Where'd you ever put that thing?"

"The last I seen of them, the gloves and cap were in the hall closet on the shelf," she says.

Waller leaves, and I turn to Detective York. "I can't believe this is happening. It's like a bad dream. It's a nightmare, and I want to wake up."

"Take it easy," he says. "We'll find out the truth. That's what we're trained to do."

The policeman returns. He shakes his head as he talks. "There was nothing down in that basement except an old table," he says. "No cot, no towels, nothing."

I jump to my feet. "That's impossible!" My heart is pounding so loudly it seems to be reverberating through the room. "One of them…" I point to Loretta. "It was you, wasn't it, who sneaked down there when Zack brought me upstairs? You cleaned up and put things away!"

"Don't say that!" Loretta screams back at me. Her face is white. She's terrified.

"But she…" I realize I am tugging at Detective York's sleeve, shaking his arm up and down in my urgency.

He puts a restraining hand on my arm, and

I turn as Bill Waller comes through the doorway. He is holding one ski mask. "This was in the closet," he says. "Just the one. I couldn't find a second one."

"Listen, please, listen," I stammer. "They might have just used one. I only saw one of them at a time. Maybe they traded off the mask with each other." I know I must be right, but my reasoning sounds lame.

Zack stands there, grinning at me. "You aren't going to weasel out of this one and leave us to take all the blame."

"The money is divided into halves," Detective York says. "Can you give me a reason for that?"

"Because one half was for her," Zack says.

"No!" I shout. "There is a third person in this scheme. I know there is! But it isn't me! Zack isn't smart enough to think up this whole plan!"

"Yeah?" Zack says, eyes glittering. "Then who is this third person?"

My legs suddenly feel so weak I have to sit down. I flop into the nearest chair and lean back in it. "I don't know," I whisper.

"See, what'd I tell you!" Zack crows.

"There *is* a third person," I repeat. "There has to be."

"We can take them downtown now," Detective York says to his partner. "Will you call the mobile crime lab? We'll need fingerprints, and so forth."

"Fingerprints?" I sat upright like a coiled spring that has been sprung. "My fingerprints are all over the house. Zack made me turn on light switches and touch glasses and furniture and all that! He *made* me do it!"

No one answers me. Zack merely gloats. Loretta stares at the wall, fingers knotted together so tightly that her knuckles look like bleached knobs of flesh.

Detective York issues instructions, and two of the policemen leave with Zack and Loretta. York gives Loretta's gun to his partner, who goes out to meet the crime lab. He holds out a hand to me, and I take it, grateful for the support. It's incredible how difficult it is to get up from the chair.

I look into Detective York's eyes as though I could discover what he is thinking, but his thoughts are closed. I am all alone.

"Zack and Loretta are lying," I tell him. "Somebody has to believe me!"

He nods slowly. He is a slow-moving, quiet man. Everything he does seems deliberate. "Think hard, Christina. Is there anything else you can tell me that might help prove your innocence?"

I try to think, but my mind is a jumble of thoughts, none of them even remotely connected. Through it all comes the whimper, "I want my mother." I'm glad I can keep it inside, to myself. What would he think of me?

"I don't know," I whisper.

"Let's go down to the basement," York tells me. "Maybe if we're there, your memory will pick up something that's important. It sometimes happens like that."

There is still a touch of doubt in his voice. I can't miss it. He is doing everything he can to help me, but he doesn't quite believe me.

I lead the way to the basement and down the stairs. The rough board railing seems more rickety than ever. "Over there..." I point to a spot against the wall. "That's where the cot was, and a small table, too."

"What did you do when you were down here?"

"I sat on the cot, or I exercised. Zack brought me a book, because I asked him to. It's the only book they had in the house, I guess."

"What kind of book?"

"One of those Gothic romances."

"What was the name?"

I can only stare at him, my mind refusing to work. "I have no idea. I couldn't keep my mind on the story. I can't even tell you what it was about."

"Did you try to get out of this basement?"

"Oh, yes!" I tell him. "You see, I figured out who the man was, but I couldn't let him know that I knew, because I was afraid he would kill me. But I recognized his voice. Then I found out by accident, when I was examining that old furnace over there, that I could hear Zack and Loretta when they were talking in the kitchen. Their voices were carried through one of the register vents and amplified inside the heater. So I listened and..."

I stop. It's coming back in a rush, and I'm eager to tell him, but I want to choose my words carefully so it doesn't sound as though I'm just babbling.

"And what?" he asks.

"Loretta was scared. She told Zack that she was afraid they would be caught, and he told her it was fixed so that if they were unlucky enough not to get away with the money, they wouldn't be charged with kidnapping."

"Did he say how this was going to be accomplished?"

"No. That's all he told her. But I know there is someone else involved. Loretta said something about Zack being talked into another crazy scheme, but he said this one was foolproof. Doesn't that sound as though someone else planned it for them?"

He doesn't respond to my question. He merely says, "You were going to tell me about trying to get out."

"Oh…of course. The heater. I took off the latch. The screw was old, and I could take it out with my fingers. And I took the latch and waited until it was late and I thought they would be asleep. It was last night."

"What time?"

"I don't know. My watch stopped."

"It's broken?"

I automatically look at my watch. I remember that after my bath Loretta gave it to me, and I put it on without thinking. Force of habit. It's running.

He takes my arm, turning it so that he can look at the face of the watch. "I see that you've reset it."

"No. I didn't. Someone else must have. I don't know…" Everything I say sounds like a dumb excuse—the kind of story little children make up when they're accused of getting into their mother's face powder, or stealing cookies, and they think they can wish the whole episode away.

"When they took me upstairs so I could clean up, they must have set my watch, and…" Tears come to my eyes again. What's the matter with me? I rarely cry. I hate to cry. And here I am, spending most of the time sobbing like a dumbbell instead of trying to tell this detective what happened.

I take a deep breath and wipe away the tears with the back of my hands. "I'll get to that part later," I say. "Right now I'll tell you about the latch. I got it loose and went up the stairs over there and tried to chip away at the door latch. It was hard to do in the dark; and the latch was clumsy and not sharp enough, and it didn't do any good."

"That's it?"

"There was no way out. I just came back to the cot and finally went to sleep."

"Let's go upstairs," he tells me. This time he goes ahead of me and stops at the top of the stairs to examine the door frame.

I watch him, holding my breath, as he stops and picks up a couple of flakes of paint. He pulls out a handkerchief and folds them into it.

"You see!" I am almost shouting, and I try to get myself under control.

"I see that something has chipped away at the paint here," he says. "Where is this latch now?"

"In my sweater pocket. I took it off and…"

There is a long pause, and he asks, "Where is the sweater?"

"I don't know. The clothes I took off weren't on the floor where I threw them when I came out of the bathtub." Quickly I tell him what happened when Zack led me around the house and Loretta came in with the gun while I took my bath. Men are moving around. Through the partially open doorway to the kitchen I can see someone working on the kitchen cabinets. I've watched enough detective programs on television to know that he is dusting for fingerprints.

"Could they get my fingerprints from the furnace, too, please?" I ask Detective York.

"Of course," he says. He motions me into the kitchen and says, "Charlie, when you're finished there, could you pick up some prints from the furnace down there—around the door especially?"

"Sure," the man called Charlie says. He looks at me speculatively. I guess everyone has heard by now what I'm accused of. Again I feel close to panic, but I fight back the terror.

"Show me the room you say they took you to," York tells me.

So we go up the stairs and to the first bedroom on the right. It's as neat as it was before, with my things still on the dresser. The dirty clothes aren't in sight.

"Maybe she put them into a hamper some-where," I say.

"What does your sweater look like?" he asks me, and I tell him.

Detective York goes to the door and calls to a policeman at the foot of the stairs. He tells him to look for the sweater. The policeman calls back to him that they found a folding cot be-hind some boxes in the closet under the stairs.

"Is there anything else you've thought of that you can tell me?" he asks when he returns.

I try to think, but I'm only aware of the fact that the house has the clinging odors of stale cooking, that somewhere outside the window is a murmuring of voices that rise and fall, out of rhythm and out of harmony with each other. Footsteps plod through the rooms. It's all part of another world—not this one I'm trapped in.

"Did you overhear Zack and Loretta say anything else?"

"The first time I heard them, he was com-plaining about her ironing all the time. She irons everything. She even irons the sheets and towels. It's funny. Ironing the sheets makes them smell cleaner. I don't know why. It's just that I noticed it with the sheets on the basement cot where I slept."

"You didn't sleep in this bed at all?"

"No." The thought hits me. "No! I didn't! And the sheets will prove it! Those muslin sheets get wrinkled when they're used. I can show you that these haven't been used at all!"

I get to the bed in two long strides and throw back the spread, blanket, and top sheet in one wide swoop. The sheets are perfectly smooth, with the fold lines still in them. I jump up and down like a little child, grabbing Detective York's shoulder. "You see," I am shouting and laughing at the same time.

He puts an arm around my shoulders and says, "Calm down. It's not much to go on."

"Why? What are you talking about? It proves what I've been telling you, doesn't it?"

"It proves only one thing—that the bed is freshly made."

A policeman comes to the door, holding out a white sweater. It's mine, but it's damp.

"I found this in the washing machine," he says. "There were a bunch of things in the machine—all still wet. They haven't got a dryer—just a clothesline in the backyard."

"This is your sweater?" York asks me.

I nod. "The latch is in the pocket."

"Nothing in these pockets," the policeman says.

"Then maybe it fell into the washing machine. It's got to be someplace in there!"

"What else was in the washing machine?" Detective York asks.

"A few odds and ends of girls' clothes, a couple of sheets, and some towels."

"The things from the basement!" I say.

"Look around for a piece of metal latch," Detective York tells the policeman. "And before you go down, check the other beds upstairs. See if the sheets are wrinkled—if they've been slept in." He comes back to me. "I think it's about time we went downtown. Your parents will probably be waiting for you at the station."

I gulp. I want so much to see my mother. I'll never be able to tell her my thoughts about her, but I feel a lot closer to her than I have ever felt before. And I want to see my grandmother to tell her I'm sorry this happened to her, that I had no part in it, and I'm glad Zack and Loretta were caught. And I want to see my father.

The policeman pokes his head back in the doorway. "Double bed in the front room was slept in. That's all."

"Doesn't that prove I'm telling the truth?" I gasp.

"It's not enough to hang a case on," Detective York says. "Come with me."

He stops to talk to some people at the foot of the stairs, then leads me through the front door. I have seen the people on the lawn without realizing we'd come into contact with each other. Suddenly they are thrusting themselves into my world, and the hubbub frightens me.

In the forefront is a face I recognize. I've watched this man on national television. It occurs to me in a split second that this is the man the policeman was talking about, and now he is shoving something into my face and talking to me.

Instinctively I stop and stare back at him.

"Miss Lattimore," he is shouting into the microphone in his resonant voice that seems to be straight out of diction school, "we were informed that you were kidnapped. Then a few moments ago we were told by two of the people being brought out of this house that you had masterminded a scheme to defraud your grandmother. Would you care to comment on this?"

Detective York takes my arm. "One side, please," he says. "Miss Lattimore doesn't need to answer your questions."

Behind the newscaster I see an extra-tall boy with freckles splattered on his face, and his red hair looks as though it put up a good fight against a comb. He has the network camera on his shoulder, and stumbles as he moves in closer. He quickly catches his balance, throwing a fast look at the newscaster, who doesn't notice.

The newscaster is too intent on getting an answer from me. While newspeople from the other TV stations are crowding around, this man is more insistent than anyone else. Again he shoves that microphone into my face and shouts, "How do you feel about being in this situation?"

It's too much to take. I stop and face him. "You ask that same stupid question of everybody! Of everybody! How can I answer it? I can't! I haven't done anything wrong, and I haven't got any reason to answer your questions, and if you don't get out of my way, I'm going to sock you!"

For a moment he looks as though he has gone into shock. Then he whirls and yells, "Kelly! Back to the car!" But Kelly is standing there, camera still on, with a huge grin that makes me glad I said what I did.

Now Detective York has my arm and is propelling me through the crowd, toward his car. I haven't got time to think about the newscaster—or Kelly. Detective Waller is standing by the car. I get inside, moving quickly, and lean against the backseat, my eyes closed. I can't believe this is happening to me. Who made up this insane play and cast me in it? Was it Zack? It couldn't be Zack or Loretta. Who is this third person the police should find? I want to go home!

They take me to the downtown station, a large building covered with slabs of beige stone trimmed in highly polished red granite.

It's not an attractive building, especially in back. We get into an elevator. The light green paint is badly scarred and scratched. A short, fat woman in a faded cotton dress peers at me from a corner. A thin man in front of her wipes the sleeve of his plaid shirt across his forehead and stares straight ahead, shoulders drooping, despair in his eyes. Where is he going? What is making him so unhappy? Why should I be thinking about him? What am I going to do about my own problem?

At the third floor we get off the elevator and step into a corridor, making a sharp turn to the right. The shiny gray tiles on the walls and the speckled tan squares on the floor combine to create a drab, ugly atmosphere. No wonder the man looked so hopeless. We go past a long wooden bench that could have come from an old church, and past a double gumball machine, and through a door marked "Homicide Division" on its glass window.

I look around the room eagerly, but there are only a few men in the room, some of them seated at the gray metal desks, one typing, and one using a green phone. The walls are lined with gray metal filing cabinets that stretch from door to door and from window to window, taking every available inch of space.

I touch Detective York's arm. "My parents?" I ask.

Without answering, he moves away to talk to the man seated at a nearby desk. Detective Waller sits at another desk and begins to type hurriedly on some crisp sheets of paper.

York comes back to my side and says, "Just come with me, and we'll get some of the preliminaries out of the way."

"What preliminaries?" I ask him, but he doesn't answer until we are inside a small room. He flips on a switch, and two long bars of fluorescent light flicker and catch. There are four green vinyl-and-chrome chairs opposite another of the metal desks, an identical chair next to the desk, and one behind it. He motions me to the nearest chair, and I sit down. He sits behind the desk.

I repeat my question. "What preliminaries?"

He picks up a pad and a pen and looks into my eyes. "This is called a hold card," he says.

I'm reading the card upside down. "That

says, 'Arrest Authorization'! You're going to arrest me?"

"Calm down," he says. "This is just a formality."

"What kind of formality? First you read me my rights, and then you fill out an arrest authorization! What are you doing to me? I thought I showed you that I was telling the truth!"

He leans back in his chair. "Christina, it's my job to gather the facts in any case I'm on. I don't make the judgments. I present enough facts to the district attorney to help him make a case against the actor involved."

"Actor?"

"Our name for someone we've picked up for a crime—the person under suspicion."

"I'm under suspicion?"

"According to what Zack and Loretta Tigus said, you are under suspicion for the crime of extortion."

"But…"

"That doesn't mean you're guilty. You should know that from your government class in school. It just means that you are suspect."

"What about the things I told you about their kidnapping me?"

"Zack and Loretta Tigus are suspect, too—at the moment for the crime of extortion. They've already been interrogated and are being booked."

"They're in jail?"

"Not yet. They're probably in the identification office right now, getting photographed and fingerprinted. Then they'll go to twenty-four-hour court and either be assigned to the county jail or be set free on bail."

"My God!" I am half out of my chair. "And all this is going to happen to me?"

I am gripping the edge of his desk, and he reaches over to cover my hands with one of his. "Take it easy," he says. "We aren't here to make it hard for you. We want to help find the truth."

"The truth is that the district attorney should bring those two horrible people to trial for kidnapping me!"

"You're a bright girl," he says. "Look at our evidence. We've got your word against theirs. We've got a couple of paint flakes from a door, and so far no sign of the latch you used to make the paint chip. We have a pair of unused sheets, but no telling when the bed was changed. No real proof."

"But Zack and Loretta have no proof either."

"Zack claims to have some witnesses in the hamburger place who saw you three planning together."

I have a mental flash of those men turning to stare at me. I can see the afternoon sun patterns across the wall. I can smell the heavy grease and the pungent, sizzling onions, just as it happened.

"But I didn't plan anything with them. I mean, Zack made it look like that, but it wasn't!"

I remember something. "Did Della tell you about the woman who was at the house? About the tape on the door?"

"Yes," he says. "She told us about that right away, but she couldn't remember what the woman looked like, and she said she didn't see any tape."

"Somebody stole my clothes from the house!"

Detective Waller comes into the room and

shuts the door. He looks down at me sternly and stares at me while he's talking to Detective York. "They traced the serial number of the gun Christina was holding. The gun belongs to her father."

I think I might faint. What happens when everything begins to come and go, and voices drone into the buzzing of bees, and dark plays with light? I feel something cold and hard touching my lips. I try to turn my head away, but a large hand has a grip on the back of my neck.

"Drink this," he says, and I obey.

Slowly the room settles down. I lean back in the chair, trying to breathe.

"Put your head between your knees," York orders. He holds my shoulders down.

I murmur in a strangled voice, "Let me up. I'm all right now."

His hand moves away, and I sit up in the chair. My hands are trembling, and I can't feel my toes, but I must tell him something. "That's what the woman stole when she was in our house! We looked for obvious things, but none of us thought of looking for the gun. My father keeps it in his desk drawer, but I don't think he has ever used it!"

Detective Waller's eyes are still on me. "You think she'll be okay now?" he asks his partner.

"Sure. Go ahead," York says, so Waller leaves.

"I'm telling the truth," I say. It's the only thing I can think of. "Please believe me."

"Christina," he says, "I promise you that I'll do my best to find out the truth in this case."

"Then it's okay," I say. "Because my story is the truth."

Waller opens the door. "Someone here to see Christina."

I jump to my feet and whirl toward the door. My arms are already lifted, ready to run to my mother's arms, but I freeze, as though in slow motion, and lower my arms gradually. A portly man, in a suit that's obviously Neiman Marcus, stands in the doorway. He doesn't smile at me. He doesn't even look at me. He talks to Detective York as though I didn't exist.

"Thank you for allowing me to be present," he says. He moves into the room, shuts the door, and places a pale fur-felt Stetson on the desk. I am entranced with the gold buckle on the side of the hatband. I know real gold when I see it.

"Mr. Hennington," Detective York says, rising. "I'm pleased to see you again."

I recognize the name—Jules Hennington. He's one of the most famous attorneys in the United States, a Houston celebrity.

They go into a few minutes of talk about cases during which they've met before, while I want to scream. Where are my parents?

Finally Mr. Hennington says, "Cristabel Lattimore is my client. On her behalf I am here to talk to you about her granddaughter."

"My grandmother? Where is she?"

He glances at me appraisingly, as though I were an unfriendly witness. "Sit down, please, Miss Lattimore."

I do as he tells me. But I must know. In a tiny voice I ask, "Please tell me. Where are my parents? I thought they would be here by now."

I've seen people look at a dead cat in the street with more interest than he shows when he looks at me now. Under the smooth polish his words are chilling. "Be reasonable, Miss Lattimore. Your parents and grandmother were apprised of the facts concerning this alleged extortion attempt. On my advice they are remaining at home. Their arrival at police headquarters would simply lead to even more damaging publicity."

I am having trouble absorbing what he is telling me. "Not even my mother? My mother isn't coming here to be with me?"

"I said," he repeats in a no-nonsense voice, "they aren't coming."

[SEVEN]

I CAN SEE how this man got his reputation for commanding juries. He seems to grow another foot in height as he stares at me, and the firmness of his tone forces me to cringe back into my chair and keep my mouth shut, though I want desperately to question him.

Mr. Hennington, apparently satisfied that I won't irritate him further, turns to Detective York. "My client, Mrs. Lattimore, phoned me immediately when she was apprised of the situation." He looks at his watch, and I look, too, hypnotized.

"I left a very important political dinner at the River Oaks Country Club," he says. "I'd like this to be taken care of as quickly as possible. In short, Mrs. Lattimore is withdrawing charges against her granddaughter, and Zack and Loretta Tigus."

"Charges?" I can't help gasping out the word.

Detective York doesn't look at me either. "The charge of extortion?"

"Of course," Mr. Hennington says.

"Miss Lattimore claims she was kidnapped," Detective York says.

"We have no time for that nonsense." Mr. Hennington gives a peremptory wave of one hand.

"I'm inclined to believe we should check out her story."

Mr. Hennington looks at me sharply and back to Detective York. "On what evidence?"

Detective York slowly sits down again, swiveling his chair around and leaning back before he answers. "At the moment we have very little to go on, but that's what our business is all about—detecting, investigating, uncovering the evidence."

"I have already spoken to the district attorney," Mr. Hennington says. He picks up his hat, dusting it lightly where it has touched the desktop. "You can verify what I have told you with a quick phone call."

Detective York gets to his feet. He seems angry, and his voice becomes a little quieter. My mind is going in crazy waves and strange patterns. I am afraid to ask this attorney questions, because I can't put them into words. I'm terrified that if I open my mouth to speak, I'll wail like a baby instead, so I'm awfully glad when Detective York speaks for me.

"Do you and your client realize that the media are on top of this in a big way? That they have the story now from Zack and Loretta that Christina was not kidnapped, but planned this venture to get hold of her grandmother's money? You want things to hang at this point?"

"It is precisely because of this unfortunate publicity in the news media that we want this situation to be ended as quickly as possible." Mr. Hennington's voice is formal. "Miss Lattimore should be grateful that her grandmother is not pressing charges."

I jump up. This is too much to take. "You actually believe that I was involved in this! You do!" I am shouting, and my whole body is trembling, but I can't stop. "I keep trying to tell everyone! I was kidnapped! I was kept in a basement! Why can't you believe me?"

He ignores what I say. "One of my assistants is preparing the necessary papers," he tells Detective York. "I'll arrange to take her home to her parents before I return to my dinner meeting." He looks at his watch again.

"No!" I shout. I want to say more, but Detective York, in one smooth movement, is around the side of the desk and is gripping my shoulder.

He speaks to Mr. Hennington, and his voice is tight. "I don't think you'd care to wait until all the paperwork is done. I'll take the responsibility of getting Miss Lattimore home safely."

There is one instant in which I can see the hesitation in Mr. Hennington's eyes. Then he nods. "That will be satisfactory," he says. "Thank you."

As he brushes past me, I say, "If someone would just pay attention to my side of this whole thing..." But again he ignores me.

Detective York shuts the door and turns toward me.

"I hate that man!" I explode. "And I hate my grandmother! Why would she do this to me?"

"Sometimes it's easier not to try to understand people," he says.

"But she must know what people will think about me! Who's going to believe me?"

"Your friends will believe you."

"Do you really think so?"

He pats my shoulder awkwardly. "You're in a tough situation, Christina. I think you've got enough guts to live through it. And I'll do what I can to help."

He goes around the desk and picks up the phone, punching the numbers with a big finger.

"You mean you'll keep investigating?"

"Whatever I can. You realize that this isn't my only case? That I handle a dozen or more cases a week?"

"Do you solve them all?"

"Not by a long shot. They only do that in the movies."

He begins to talk to someone, and I sit on the edge of the chair, waiting, my back feeling as though a wooden coat hanger has been shoved along my backbone to hold it together.

When he hangs up, he shrugs. "I said I'll do what I can. I don't know how much that will be. That's all I can promise you."

"I don't want to go home," I tell him. "I want you to put me in jail. I want to go to court and make people realize that Zack and Loretta are lying!"

He sits opposite me and leans forward on the desk. "Look, Christina, in the first place we haven't got enough evidence on those two on a kidnapping charge to arrest them. They had to be booked on the extortion charge. The district attorney has to have real evidence in order to prosecute them on a kidnapping charge, and to be brutally honest with you, the evidence is too slim to build a case. It comes down to your word against theirs."

"But the ransom note. I deliberately misspelled my name. That must prove something."

"It only proves that a note was sent. On the witness stand Zack and Loretta would say you had misspelled your name to make it look like a real kidnapping." He leans back in his chair again and adds, "The DA won't prose-cute on this extortion thing if his plaintiff backs out. He can't waste the time or money on a case he's bound to lose."

"My grandmother is the plaintiff?"

"It's her money that was taken. Yes, she's the plaintiff—or was. Now the case is thrown out, and it's all over except taking you home."

"It's all over for everyone but me."

He nods.

"When does my nightmare end?"

Detective York stands up, and I stand, too. The room seems smaller than before, and too warm, so that my back has become sticky damp against the slick vinyl chair.

"I think it's going to be up to you when the nightmare is over," he says. "Some people have nightmares that never end. But you—I think you'll make it through yours. It will just take time."

"And you'll help me."

"Whatever I can do. It won't be much."

I can't answer. All of a sudden I'm terribly tired, too tired to talk. "Can we leave now?"

I turn toward the doorway. I'm so tired,

and all I want is to go home. My mother will believe me. If I cling to this thought, I'll be all right.

We go through the homicide room. Detective Waller says, "The press is downstairs by the elevator. I sent word not to let them come up here."

"Thanks," Detective York says. "We'll take the back stairs."

He doesn't tell his partner that he's taking me home. I guess he doesn't need to. They seem to work together like two people who have known each other for a long time. Maybe they read each other's minds.

He takes my arm and hurries me through the stairwell, where voices echo in hollow shouts from unseen places, bouncing against the bleak walls. Soon we are outside, through the parking lot, and in his car. No one has followed us.

On the drive home he tries to talk to me, but it's too much effort to answer. Part of my mind doesn't believe what is happening to me, and the other part is staring into a long, dark tunnel and wants to scream it open. Nothing else registers.

The car swings into the drive in front of my home. I'm acutely aware of the look of my home in the twilight shadows, as though my sense of sight has outdistanced the others. It's as though I were seeing my home after a long, long time. In a way I'm surprised that it looks the same as it always has. A fat squirrel skims the drive in front of the car in a brown flash, and I am jolted back to a sense of normalcy—whatever that has been for me.

Detective York parks the car in front of the veranda.

"Thanks," I say, reaching out to open the door.

He offers me a smile, and I accept it as something to cling to. "Not so fast," he says. "I'm coming inside with you."

"Will my parents be there?" Maybe he knows. After all that has happened to me, I don't know.

"Yes," he says. "They've been waiting for you."

"How do you know all these things?"

"Our office was in contact with them by telephone. Surely you teenagers know what telephones are?"

I know he's trying to cheer me up, but I am not ready for cheerfulness. I open the door on my side of the car and climb out, leading the way up the steps. I see a flutter of the curtain in one of the front windows, and before I can reach the door, it is thrown open. My mother rushes out, her arms opened wide to me.

Everything spills over. I run to my mother, hugging her, feeling her arms wrap around me like protective padding to shut out the world, to keep all harm away from me. We are both crying and hugging, with nothing to stop us. Oh, Mother, Mother, Mother. I'm so glad you're here!

As though our energies are blended together, as one we shut off the tears, sniffing, holding each other tightly, fumbling for tissues. We stand back, looking at each other. My mother is still gripping my shoulders as though she would never let me go.

"Oh, Mother," I sigh. "I'm so glad to be home again."

A look of pain twists her face as it passes like a swell in the ocean. "Oh, Christina," she says, "you foolish, foolish girl! Why did you do it?"

I am numb. I can only stare at her. When I manage to speak, my voice comes out in a croak. "I was kidnapped. Don't you believe me?"

"But they told us..."

"Don't you know me, Mother?" Anger is bringing back my strength. "Don't you know I wouldn't do anything to hurt Cristabel?"

Her hands flutter to her face. "Christina, I was only going by what the police told us—that those...people...whom they arrested said you had planned everything. That's even the way it's been told on the television news."

"But I was sure my own mother would believe me!" It's growing dark quickly, and I hear a tree frog's guttural, rhythmic mating call. The air is damp with a musty, cloying odor.

Detective York steps to my side, and I realize he has been patiently waiting at the bottom of the veranda steps. He introduces himself to my mother and says, "May we go inside, please? I'd like to talk to you."

"Of course, of course," my mother stammers. She leads the way, then steps behind us to close the door. I walk resolutely into the living room, where I know my father will be waiting. Once, when I was in the fifth grade, I was accidentally hit in the stomach with a baseball bat and lost my breath. It was an awful experience, so terrible that I can still remember how it felt. I feel the same way now.

He comes to meet me. He quickly bends his head down against mine, wrapping me in a smothering hug. But I have seen the tears in his eyes.

"We're glad to have you home again, Christina," he says.

Rosella's head is bobbing up and down like the head on a little windup toy. "I couldn't leave until I knew you were safely home," she tells me. "I canceled my trip."

"We prayed for your safe return," my father says. He stands back and looks at me. They are all looking at me.

"Thank you," I say. "Now will you please pray that I'll be able to prove my innocence?"

I don't think he hears me. It's as though he had worked out in advance what he is going to say. "Christina, we'll have a long talk about this situation. It's important that you make peace with your grandmother."

I have my mouth open to reply when once again I feel a strong hand pressing down on my shoulder. Detective York steps to my side.

"I think that first I had better speak my piece," he says. "I'm Detective York and am in charge—*was* in charge—of this case before Mrs. Lattimore dropped the charges."

My father is gracious, and my mother remembers her manners. Soon we are all seated in the living room, and Detective York has turned down a polite offer of coffee or tea.

"I'm sorry that the case was closed so quickly," he tells them. "As it stands now, we have only Christina's word against the word of Zack and Loretta Tigus. If we had been allowed to dig into things, maybe my partner and I could have come up with something that would have helped to clear Christina's name."

"I don't know what to say." My father looks helpless, almost frightened. "My mother feels it's better to let the matter die down as quickly as possible. She feels this is a source of great embarrassment."

"Good God!" I explode. "I'm kidnapped and held in a cold basement, scared to death, and you say it's a source of embarrassment! What kind of father are you?"

He looks at me sadly. "Christina, please, don't take the name of the Lord in vain."

There's a funny expression on Rosella's face, as though she wished she could laugh aloud, but as she sees me watching her, she quickly stares at the floor.

My mother moves to perch on the sofa beside me and pats my arm. "You're exhausted, dear. In the morning things will look much, much better. Right now it's like a bad dream, but a good night's sleep will help. Maybe your father could talk to Cristabel."

"Tomorrow the Houston *Post* will have the story," my father says. "Tonight there was just a bare mention in the *Chronicle* because of the timing, I suppose. Naturally, it was on the front page. There is no way to stop the journalists from printing the story."

Della comes to the doorway. "Mr. Lattimore, there's a reporter on the phone, and he..." She stops, staring at me. Then a wide smile creases her chubby face. "Christina! Nobody told me you were here already! I'm so glad to see you back home again! We was worried to death!"

"Thank you, Della," I say.

"Tell the reporter we are not available," my father says. Della leaves, heading back to the telephone.

Detective York speaks up. "This is a difficult time for all of you, I understand," he says. "I'd like to go over the facts as we know them, to help you get a fuller picture of what happened to your daughter."

"Oh, dear! I'm not sure I want to go through all that." My mother sighs.

"Please listen," I ask them.

There is silence, and Detective York takes the initiative. He goes over what I told him and what Zack and Loretta said. He tells them about the missing latch to the furnace, and the paint chipped at the door to the basement. He even tells them about the unused, freshly ironed sheets. Finally he pauses.

"But they had already divided the money into two parcels," my father says. "Why would they do that if Christina weren't to get her share?"

"Because there was someone else involved! Someone who planned it for them!" I say.

I look around the room. Rosella has a little crease of indecision between her eyes. My mother looks as though she wants to burst into tears again. My father is frowning. Della is standing in the doorway, and her face is deliberately blank. They are trying to reconcile the information we have given them with what they were told before.

Detective York gets slowly to his feet. "Our police department is badly understaffed. We don't have nearly enough detectives for a city of this size, and I'm always working under an overload of cases. I would like to help Christina, and maybe I will be able to turn up something. We never know when an informer from one case will lead us back to another case with vital information. However, I'd like to suggest that if you want to help your daughter prove her innocence, you hire a private investigator who can do justice to the job. I can give you a couple of names to call."

"Oh," my mother says. "We could do that, couldn't we?" She keeps her eyes on my father's face.

"I—I think we'd better discuss this with my mother," my father says. He rises and leads the way toward the front hallway. "I appreciate your suggestion, but my mother expressly stated that it would be better to let this affair die down as quickly as possible."

Detective York's glance at me is one of pity. I smile at him and walk to his side. "May I have your card, please? I'll want to know where to get in touch with you. Because I'm not going to give up on this, not even if I have to do the detective work myself."

"I'd advise against it," he says. "You don't know how dangerous it can be working with people of this type." But he gives me his card.

Detective York turns to my father. "I understand that you do a lot of preaching."

My father perks up. "Yes," he says. "Perhaps you've been to one of my seminars?"

"No," York says, shaking his head. "I'm afraid that with my hours I don't have time for things like that."

"We can always find time to discover the word of the Lord."

Detective York nods. "I'm familiar with the

Bible. As a matter of fact, I'm thinking of an apt quotation right now."

"And what is that?"

He looks my father straight in the eyes as though he would bore through to the brain if he could. "Judge not, that ye be not judged," he says. Then he turns and marches through the hallway. I hear the front door close firmly.

Della gives a snuffled snort and scurries off toward the kitchen. Rosella whispers, "I'll check those papers in the office," and disappears. My mother bustles around, plumping pillows and trying to pretend she hasn't heard.

I say to my father, noting that his face has reddened, "Detective York could have given me a quotation, too. One on forgiveness. I know I should forgive you, but right now I can't. I can't forgive you for not believing in me enough to want to help me."

I follow the path Della took toward the kitchen, but my father says, "Where are you going? There are still things to talk about."

"Not now, Daddy," I say. "Nobody asked me if I was hungry, and I haven't had anything to eat for most of the day."

"Oh, darling," my mother says. "I didn't think! Let me get something for you."

"I'd rather get it myself, Mother. You stay here. Daddy needs you to talk to him."

It's the first time I've ever seen anyone challenge my father. I suppose there's never been anything to challenge him about. In a way I'm delighted with Detective York for saying what he did, and in a way I'm sorry for my father, because without his facade of religion he's like a toy balloon with the air let out, that fizzles around until it lies flat and useless.

I am halfway to the kitchen when the doorbell rings, and rings again. I hear voices and my father's angry, firm voice answering that I will not speak to the press under any conditions. Oh, Daddy, why can't you say, "Because our daughter is innocent of those charges!"?

Della has left the kitchen. Maybe she's gone home by now. I'm hungry and want to eat something, but now I can't. A large fist inside my throat is squeezing, and a fire is burning behind my eyelids. The pain is too much to take. For a long time I sit motionless in the darkness at the kitchen table, trying to live with it.

The light footsteps tap up behind me. Rosella whispers, "Christina, there is a boy here to see you. He says he's a friend."

"I don't know any boys," I tell her. "What's his name?"

"T. J. Kelly, he says."

I frown in concentration. "I don't know a Kelly."

"Shall I tell him to go away?"

I shake my head. "No," I say. "I'll find out what he wants. Where are Mother and Daddy?"

"In your father's office. They're on the phone with Cristabel. Your mother wants to give you a chance to relax and eat in peace. Then they'll probably want to talk to you." She looks at the bare table. "But you haven't eaten anything."

"I can't yet," I say.

"Della's left for the day," she says, "so I let this Kelly in, and he's waiting for you in the living room."

"Thanks, Rosella."

She moves away hesitantly, tossing me quick, birdlike glances over her shoulder. I stand up, steady myself, and go to the living room to see who and what this "Kelly" is all about.

As I come to the doorway, he turns, and an elbow hits a crystal vase, sending it spinning. Kelly neatly catches it in time and rights it on the table. Then he grins at me. "Hi," he says. "I don't think you'll remember me. I'm T. J. Kelly."

I remember him all right. With that wild red hair and all those freckles, such a tall guy would stand out in any crowd. But when I saw him he was behind a camera.

I take a step backward. "Oh, no. You told Rosella you were my friend, but you came to get an interview. Right?"

"Wrong. I'm just a sophomore at the University of Houston, majoring in communications and manning a camera part-time to help pay my tuition. I'm not a reporter."

"Then why did you come?"

"For a couple of reasons," Kelly says. "I wanted to thank you for telling off that New York transplant who thinks he knows all there is to know about television newscasting. It was time someone put him in his place. Working for him is a real pain."

"I don't ever want to see that man again."

"You won't have to."

"Well, look," I say. I can feel Rosella listening in the doorway. I should have known someone would be keeping an eye on me. "Would you like a sandwich or something?"

He holds up a hand. "Wait a minute. I didn't finish telling you the reason why I came to see you."

I just look at him, waiting to hear what he's going to say.

"I came to tell you," Kelly says, "that I believe you."

[EIGHT]

A S MY mind finally registers what Kelly has told me, my last defenses crumble. "Then you're the only one," I whisper. "You're the only one who really believes me."

I don't want to cry again, but there's nothing I can do to stop it. I cover my face with my hands and sob. I feel Kelly put his arms gingerly around my shoulders and hold me, as though he's used to breaking things and wants to be very careful. I lean against his chest until the tears dry up. I find I am using a handkerchief that smells something like gasoline, but I don't mind.

"Kelly…" I mumble.

"Blow your nose, so you'll stop sniffling," Kelly says.

I do as he tells me. "I'm sorry I cried," I say, embarrassed. I know my eyes are red and puffy and I must look a mess.

"It's okay," Kelly says. "I've got four sisters. I've seen girls cry a lot."

I can't help giggling, and I realize it's the first time I've laughed in a long, long time. It's been days, but it feels like years.

I take Kelly out to the kitchen and fix us some ham sandwiches. Kelly likes mustard and lots of pickle relish in his, so I make mine that way, too. With big glasses of milk, they taste better than anything I've ever eaten. Maybe it's just that I'm glad I want to eat again.

"If you weren't so skinny," Kelly says, wiping pickle juice off his shirt, "you'd really be good-looking."

I think about that a moment. "Is that supposed to be a compliment?"

"No," Kelly says.

"Then what?"

"It's okay," Kelly says, taking a long gulp of milk. "If you were really good-looking I wouldn't be here. Fantastic-looking girls scare me."

I start to giggle again. "You're kind of skinny yourself, you know."

"I know," he says. "It's because I grew so fast. I'm still growing, too. It makes it hard to get clothes on sale. Not many stores carry extra-longs."

He munches contentedly on his last sandwich, and I say, "Kelly, could I tell you what happened?"

"I want you to," he says.

So I go into the whole thing, right up to Detective York's leaving our house. I leave out what he said to my father.

Kelly nods, wipes his mouth with a paper napkin, and says, "Where do we start?"

"We? You mean you want to help me?"

"Why not?"

"Why? Well, because you don't really know me."

"When you came out of that house, you looked scared to death, the way a victim looks. People who are caught breaking laws look scared, too, but in a different way, a kind of defiant way."

"I'm still scared."

"It's going to be okay," Kelly says.

"Detective York wanted my parents to hire a private investigator. I'm pretty sure they won't. I told him I'd investigate this thing myself, but he said that I shouldn't, that it would be dangerous." I feel I must tell him this.

"Okay," Kelly says. "But if you're the only one who's going to do anything to try to prove your innocence, then you're going to need some help. When you've got yourself put together, I'll be here."

What I feel like saying is, "Kelly, I think I'm in love with you!" But I can't, so I say, "Thanks, Kelly. I think I'm getting myself put together now."

Kelly stands up, and his head grazes the glass-balled light fixture that hangs low over the kitchen table. He grabs it and stops its erratic swing.

"I'll come by tomorrow evening, if it's all right with you," he says. "I've got morning classes and work for the station on the mobile unit all afternoon."

"I'll be here. I don't think I'm going anywhere tomorrow."

"Except to school."

"I mean school in particular. I don't want to go."

"If you don't go, they'll take it as a sign you're guilty of those charges," Kelly says. "What you've got to do is go and make the best of it."

I think about facing everyone, and I shudder. "I don't think I can."

"Sure you can," Kelly says. "You've got to. Talk to your friend, Lorna. See if she remembers anything suspicious about Zack and Loretta. You said she always goes to that hamburger place with you."

Kelly's right. I can't hide. I'd never get anything done. I walk with him to the door, and lean against it, thinking about him, after he leaves. There's one person who really believes in me—just one. My mother is wavering. My father believes what Cristabel tells him to believe. Oh, Detective York is keeping an open mind, so I can count him in a way. I wonder why Lorna hasn't called.

I go to my father's study. Rosella has left for the day, and he sits at his desk in a pool of sharp light beamed down from a crook-necked lamp. He looks old and tired. There are dark bags under his eyes, and for a moment I feel sorry for him.

"You and Mother wanted to talk to me, Daddy."

He looks up. "Rosella said you were entertaining a guest. There was not much point in waiting for you, since your mother had a sick headache. I sent her to bed. She's probably asleep by now."

"Rosella said you were phoning Cristabel."

"We were unable to reach her."

I hesitate. "No one phoned me," I finally manage to say. It sounds inane.

"No one could have phoned," he says. "We have the phones off the hook."

"Oh."

"Were you expecting a call?"

"I thought maybe Lorna."

"You'll see her tomorrow in school. It's best not to accept any calls tonight."

"Daddy, what was it like here while I was gone? What did you all do?"

"Do?" he echoes.

"You know. Did you call the police? Did you talk to any reporters? Did Zack bring

Cristabel a note at her office or her home or what? What went on?"

He sighs. "It's hard to describe. It seemed as though everything was happening at once, but in a way it wasn't happening fast enough. There were long periods of waiting and worrying and praying, of course. And we talked to various policemen—not that Detective York, but a man with a mustache—Walker or Waller, something like that. And we held a family meeting so Cristabel could decide what we should do. We did manage to keep the press out of it. The whole thing was a horrible experience."

"Are you glad I'm home, Daddy?" His office smells tidily clean, like a mixture of lemon wax and disinfectant. He is beginning to bald. There is a shiny spot at the crown of his head, collecting and reflecting the light. Why did I ask that question?

The question surprises him as much as it does me. "Of course I'm glad," he says. "I just wish the circumstances were happier."

I take a deep breath and clench my fists. "It's very hard to be kidnapped under *happy* circumstances, Daddy." Quickly, I turn and go upstairs to my room. I would like to say good night to my mother, but her room is dark, and I suppose she must be asleep. I didn't know it was possible to be hurt to the point of agony, but that's the way I feel.

I automatically bathe, brush my hair, and climb into bed. I pull the blankets up to my chin and curl up on my side in my usual comfortable fetal position, which has begun to make an imprint in the mattress. This is my own bed. I am home safely, and for now that's all that counts.

In my sleep I dream that I am clinging tightly to Kelly's hand. I think I cling to it all through the night, because when I wake in the morning my right fist is tightly clenched.

But morning is so unreal. As the sun seeps through the curtains, so do memories seep into my conscious mind. It's my own bed…it's the basement…my bed. I sit up, trying to orient myself, pushing away the tangled hair that falls in front of my eyes. I have always thought it was the pits in old-fashioned books to have some character say, "Where am I?" But now I know where they're coming from. It takes me a few minutes to get myself into perspective.

Same old room, same frilly curtains, same canopied bed. But not the same me. I'm a different person now. I'll never be the same again.

Della doesn't usually come this early. Often I pass her as I'm driving to school, and she's walking from the bus stop, leaning into each puffing, deliberate step. My mother is in the kitchen, making French toast. She smiles brightly at me and keeps up a happy chatter. She's making my favorite breakfast, and each time she passes me she touches my shoulder, or smooths back my hair, or pats my cheek. My mother is telling me that she loves me. How can you love someone—really love her—and not trust her? But I badly need the love she offers me, and I take it greedily. "Mother," I say, "I thought about you when I was in that basement alone."

She sits at the table next to me, cradling her coffee cup, spots of red on her cheeks.

"It was cold in that basement, and dark, and awful scary. I could hear roaches. Did you ever hear a roach in the dark and wonder where it was going?"

She shudders. "No," she says.

For a moment we sit quietly. Then I pull

my mind back to its original track. "Anyhow, I thought about you and how pretty you are. I think it was the first time that I ever really looked at you, and I was looking at you in my mind."

"Oh, Christina," she says. She pats my hand nervously, and I see there are tears in her eyes.

"Someday I'll tell you what it was like, being kidnapped. I just realized that no one in the family has asked me what it was like, or how I felt, or what happened to me."

"But…" The sentence dies. She presses her lips together and blinks rapidly.

I hunch my shoulders against the blow of what she would have said. "You didn't ask because no matter what you told me, there were too many doubts. You didn't really believe my story." I leave the French toast half eaten and push back my chair quickly. "I've got to leave for school."

"Don't you want the rest of your breakfast? I made your favorite."

"Thanks, Mother. It was very good. I just don't have time now."

We talk to each other in useful platitudes as I get my books together. What we have said to each other I don't know, because my mind has moved ahead to what will happen when I arrive at Madame DeJon's. It's like anticipating a visit to the dentist's when a filling has fallen out and you've got a cavity as big as the tip of your tongue. The anticipation can be torture, often worse than the reality. Maybe this will be the same. Kelly said I'd have to go to school. Detective York said I'd make it through the tough days. I guess I'll have to find out.

But it's bad. I pull into the parking lot, and two men leap toward my car.

One of them is pulling out identification and introducing himself. They're from two of the news services. They bend to peer through the car window.

"Go away," I tell them, rolling the window down another inch.

"Wouldn't you like to give us your version of the story?"

"Why should I?"

"We have stories from Zack and Loretta Tigus. Have you seen the morning paper?"

"No."

"Wasn't it a pretty desperate attempt to get money from your grandmother? Did you really think it would work?"

"I was not involved with those two weirdos! I was not trying to get money from my grandmother. Zack and Loretta kidnapped me, and they set the whole thing up so this would be their safety valve in case they couldn't get away with the money."

"You're sticking to this story?" the man closest to the window asks.

"It's the truth."

I have been trying to keep my feelings under control, but now I'm furious. I throw open the door to my car, giving his knees a good crack. He stumbles backward into the other reporter. I get out of the car, quickly lock the door, and say, "You have your minds made up. It won't make any difference what I say. Your story is going to be slanted and biased and prejudiced and a bunch of lies. My story is the truth, and that's why I'm sticking to it. Now get lost, or I'll call the police and tell them you're harassing me!"

"Now, look," one of them says. "Our jobs…"

But I turn and run toward the building. There are other cars arriving—a few more latecomers like me—and the girls are staring strangely at the men. As I reach the back door of Madame DeJon's administrative building, I glance over my shoulder and see them getting into their car. What good does it do to talk to reporters if they're going to write the story from their predetermined viewpoint, instead of giving the facts as they stand?

It's almost time for class, and some of the girls are busy with lockers and books and stuff as I come by. A few people I thought were my friends avoid meeting my eyes and don't speak to me. A few gulp out, "Hi, Christina," the way they'd spit pits from prunes. I keep my shoulders back and my head up, just like in the old movie where Ronald Colman goes to the guillotine. Where is Lorna?

I open the door to English, and she is there, rearranging clippings on the bulletin board. No one else is in the room yet.

"Lorna," I say, standing there, looking at her, waiting for her to react. My best friend. What is she going to do?

Lorna turns, sees me, and runs to hug me

"Oh, Christina! It was terrible, not knowing where you were or what was happening! I knew something was wrong by the way your parents acted when I phoned you, but no one would tell me what it was. I didn't know if you were terribly sick, or what in the world happened!"

"They didn't tell you anything?"

"I guess they were trying to keep it quiet. Your mother did call Saturday morning and ask to talk to you. I just figured she thought you had come back to my house. I didn't get the picture until later, and then I wondered..."

"Wondered what?"

"Well, I remembered how upset you were about not being able to go with the class on that trip to France, and I thought you might have run away from home."

For a moment it doesn't register. I had forgotten about the class trip. It shocks me that just a few days ago it was so important to me. Now I couldn't care less. I look directly into Lorna's eyes.

"But you know now that I was kidnapped."

"Yes," she says, but there is a quick flicker

in her eyes, and her gaze shifts to a spot over my left ear.

"You have to believe me, Lorna."

She moves to the bulletin board and puts in a few pins. "I've got to have this ready before class starts."

"Lorna…"

She turns. "Detective York came to see me last night. He explained everything that happened. He told me your side of the story, and he asked me if I had any information at all that would help. He thought I could verify what you said happened at Zack's hamburger place."

"Could you?"

She shakes her head and holds out her hands, palms up. "You know I couldn't!" Her voice comes out in a wail. "Christina, you didn't say one word about Zack and Loretta coming to the table to talk to you!"

"I didn't think it was important enough to talk about."

"But I'm not a mind reader! I wanted to help you, but I couldn't!"

"They followed me to your house Friday night, and then to my house."

"How in the world could I know that?"

I walk back to my desk and put my books on it. "Don't get upset, Lorna," I tell her. "It doesn't matter. The only thing that matters is that you believe me."

"Of course I believe you."

I turn and look at her carefully. Lorna, with all her polish, can't even tell a good lie.

"I'm glad," I say, but my voice sounds hollow.

"We'll get together after school," she says, offering what she can of her friendship. "Oh… but not today. I'm going shopping with my mother for some shoes. Maybe…well…we'll see how tomorrow works out."

People begin to come into the room. Mrs. Hardy bustles in with an untidy stack of papers and is in constant motion until the bell rings. She dives into English Lit. I can see what is going to happen. No one is going to acknowledge that anything out of the ordinary went on. No one is going to ask me about what I went through. They are being polite, because I am obviously an embarrassment at Madame DeJon's, where the nicest of Houston families just don't have daughters who get involved in extortion. Don't they want to know the truth? Don't they care?

The ringing of the bell comes as a complete surprise to me. I realize I haven't heard a word of what went on in class. *What am I doing here?*

I automatically stand, pulling my books into the ready-made niche in my arms. Lorna moves toward me. "I tried to phone you last night, but your line was busy."

"My father took the phone off the hook."

"I wanted to tell you that—no matter what—I was glad you're back."

"No matter what?" I stare at her.

Lorna is flustered. "Well, Detective York hadn't come by yet, and all I heard was what was on TV, and they didn't know everything." She flushes, and her words are angry. "For real, Christina, how can you expect me to know what happened when nobody told me? And for that matter, why didn't you call me?"

"I don't know."

"Well, look," she says. "I'm your friend. Why are you so edgy about everything I say?"

I attempt a smile. "Okay, Lorna. I guess I'm

just on the floor. I've never felt so down in my life."

She smiles back. "I understand, Chris." People are pushing past us now, coming into the next class, and she looks at them, startled. "We're going to be late! See you at lunch!"

I make it through the day. How, I'm not sure. At lunch I try to tell some of my friends about being kidnapped, and they listen with wide eyes, the way they'd watch a car chase on a cops-and-robbers television show. But they tell others, and the word gets around. It no longer seems to matter whether they believe me or not. I want them to know my side of the story. Now I'm sorry I didn't go into it with those reporters.

There's one more thing I must do. I want to talk to Cristabel. I drive to her office building, ride up the smoothly silent elevator, and enter the reception area. The receptionist doesn't smile at me this time. She looks up and blinks like an owl caught in bright sunlight.

"I'd like to see my grandmother, please," I tell her.

"Oh. Surely. Right away." She fumbles with the intercom, keeping her eyes on me. She acts as though she thinks I've come from robbing a bank.

There is an exchange of low murmurs, and the receptionist says, "Your grandmother is getting ready for a dinner engagement. She'll see you another time."

Maybe another time I would have bought this excuse, but not now. "It doesn't take her that long to put on her false eyelashes," I say. Without another word I open the door, go down the hallway, and barge into my grandmother's office.

Cristabel is standing behind her desk, looking out at the city, over which wisps of stark white clouds make puff marks against the blue sky. She whirls at my entrance.

"I thought..." she begins.

There are deep bluish circles under her eyes. She looks closer to her actual age.

"Why didn't you want to see me?" I ask her. "You're my grandmother, and you haven't even tried to see me after this kidnapping."

"Sit down, Christina," she says, and glides into her own leather chair. "I suppose now is as good a time to talk as any."

"I came because you must believe the

truth," I tell her. "Those people kidnapped me. They are lying when they say I had anything to do with it."

"I talked this over with my attorney," she says. "He insisted there was not a shred of proof substantiating your claim that you were kidnapped."

"Your attorney is an ass," I say. "He just wanted to get the whole thing over with as fast as possible and get back to his dinner party."

"If we're going to talk, we're going to do it without immature emotional outbursts," she says in her controlled voice.

I nod. "All right, Cristabel. Would you believe that your attorney didn't even want to talk to me? He talked over my head to the detective. He took it for granted that Zack and Loretta were telling the truth. And he didn't want to hear my side of the story, because that might confuse him."

"Christina..." she warns.

"Grandmother," I say without thinking. "Will you just let me tell you what happened from beginning to end? Please?"

She winces at the word "grandmother,"

but says, "All right. I'm willing to listen. I'll have Eleanor take any calls that might interrupt us."

As soon as she has made the necessary arrangements, she sits back in her chair. I clear my throat and begin at the very beginning and carry it through to the moment Detective York takes me home.

"Do I have to prove that I wasn't a part of the plot?" I ask her.

She is thinking. As I have talked, she has shifted to a position with her elbows resting on her desk, her chin cradled in her hands. It's her "thinking" position, and I know she is paying close attention to my words.

"Let's take this step-by-step," she says. "Why was the money divided into two piles?"

"Because there is someone else involved in this."

"Who?"

"I don't know! But someone had to be! Zack and Loretta couldn't have worked this out by themselves."

"To be honest with you, Christina, your claim seems to be a bit far-fetched."

"That's why nobody believes me."

"You are basing your proof of innocence on just two things—that the sheets on the bed had not been used, and that you had tried to open the basement door with a piece of metal that has disappeared. That's not much proof. It leaves a lot to take on faith."

I groan. "But that's what I want from you—faith! I'll find more proof. I will!"

"How?"

"Detective York suggested that Daddy hire a private investigator, but he didn't want to. I think if you told him it was all right, he would do it. He does whatever you tell him to do."

The look on her face is sheer pain, but she gets her emotions under control immediately. "Your father simply respects my good judgment," she says. "He always has."

"So if you tell him?" I'm scarcely breathing, living on hope.

Cristabel gets up and walks back and forth in front of the window wall of her office. I don't speak. I wait.

Finally she turns and says, "Christina, I don't know what an investigator could turn up that might help you. Your story is so terribly unsubstantiated. In the business world no one would put money into a venture with odds like that."

"But, Cristabel! I'm not a business!"

"Please, Christina, let's be reasonable. Hiring someone to look for evidence would only drag this thing out. It would be best for the entire family if it were dropped."

"But I came to see you to ask you not to drop it. At this point I wouldn't even mind if you preferred charges, so that this thing could come to trial and people could find out what really happened."

"You'd want to be tried on extortion charges?"

"Well...if the truth comes out, there wouldn't be a trial. Detective York would be allowed to investigate, and he'd discover the truth."

"And what if he didn't? Have you thought of that? Really, Christina, what you are asking is horrible! To drag your whole family through months and months of newspaper publicity—all of it sensational—and to have this charge against you! No! It's out of the question!"

I get to my feet. "Then, please, think of some way to help me, Cristabel."

She stands, too, and we stare at each other across the desk. With all my energy I am trying to match her strength. Finally she says, "I have given this much thought. Believe me, I have. The best thing for all of us is to have the publicity die down as quickly as possible."

"But people will always believe the worst about me!"

"That will die down, too. People will forget."

I don't know if my anguish shows, but Cristabel loses her cool. She puts her hands to her face, covering her eyes. "Go home, Christina," she says. "We'll discuss this later."

"Won't you help me? Do you want to let me take the blame for something I didn't do?"

"I can understand your attitude." Her voice trembles. "But I've worked with all my strength to build my position. I can't afford months of racking publicity, of gossip, of...I love you. I forgive you, but you should have thought. You should have known."

What she is really saying gets through to me. "You don't believe me." My voice is quiet. I am too numb to shout. What did I expect?

I don't say good-bye. I just walk out of the office, leaving my grandmother with her hands still covering her eyes, go past the receptionist, and into an elevator. The attendant in the parking garage scoops my money into his grimy hand and tells me to have a good day.

A good day? I don't even remember what a good day is.

I drive around for a while before I go home. I don't feel like talking to anyone. But finally the sun spills all over the western sky, blinding the drivers who are hurrying home from downtown, and I head for home.

A car is parked in the driveway that curves through our front yard, and I stop behind it. I'm not even curious about whose car it could be. It's pretty much of a junk car, an old Volkswagen with scratched orange paint and a few dents. Our gardener uses a better car than that to carry his tools in.

Someone is climbing out of the car, long legs stretching, unbending, as though they'd been folded away for the winter. It's Kelly, and for a moment I feel a spark of joy.

I hop out of my car, too, and meet him there in the driveway. "You're here," I say.

"I told you I would be," he answers. "Are you ready to get to work?"

"Doing what?"

"You've got to think ahead," Kelly says. "There's something important we have to do."

"What?"

"You talked about a third person being involved in the kidnapping. Don't you think the best place to start is to figure out who that third person could be?"

"You believe me," I say, my voice barely a whisper. Kelly can't possibly know how glad I am that he came along when he did.

"I believe you," he says, "and moving on from there, I believe the evidence. The money was divided into two equal halves, and Zack and Loretta aren't bright enough to have worked out the kidnapping plan. They talked a lot to the press after they were released. They're out of jail now with charges against them dropped—which you know, of course."

"Are they back in—that house?"

"Yeah."

I have to ask. "What did they say to the press? Anything new?"

"No. Same old stuff they told the police. But I'm like you. I think it adds up to zilch. Somebody smarter than they were had to figure it out. It was like an insurance policy, where if you have an accident—or, in this case, get caught with the money before you leave the country—you get off free and clear."

"Come on inside," I tell him. "We'll get something to eat, and then we'll find a quiet place to talk and see what we can come up with."

Kelly puts a hand on my arm. I like the strength in it. I like the way it feels when he touches me. "This is going to be a great experience," Kelly says. His eyes shine with excitement.

"I wouldn't call it a great experience," I tell him. "I'm a little bit scared about the whole thing. I keep remembering that Detective York said it might be dangerous for me to investigate."

Kelly runs his fingers through his tousled hair, making it look even worse, if possible. "You're scared?"

"Kidnapping is one thing. Murder is another." I shiver.

"Murder? I think you're worrying too much. But you don't have to follow through. We can let it drop."

"No way," I tell him. "I can't keep going with everyone suspecting me."

"Okay. As long as you're sure you want to get into this." He looks relieved and greatly pleased.

"I do."

"Then let's get started," Kelly says. "We'll have to work fast before...well, before whoever that third person is knows we're trying to discover his identity."

[NINE]

DELLA SERVES Kelly and me at the dining-room table, where we perch down at one end of the dark mahogany in an unbalanced island of white Madeira place mats and bone china.

"This is nice stuff," Kelly says. "Someday I'm going to live like this."

"Where do you live?" I ask him.

He waits until he's gulped down a mouthful of cheese omelet, and then says, "We live in a standard suburban home in southwest Houston. Looks like every tenth house on the block on the outside, all of them with about the same floor plan on the inside." He mentions the subdivision.

"That's a pretty area of town," I say politely. I'm uncomfortable because I hear my parents arguing.

"It's okay," he answers, "but for me, someday, it's going to get better."

I start to ask him what he's planning to do with the rest of his life, but my mother and father come in to say hello. They're on their way to a church board meeting.

They'd been arguing about going, and the argument droned on. When I say "droned," I mean their arguments get boring, because they try to be gentle with each other. My father felt that it was important they show at this meeting and act as though nothing had happened. My mother said she would die of embarrassment, and what would people think!

At one point my father referred to Cristabel's phone call, so I know she had confirmed her original decision to do or say nothing more on the subject. But neither of my parents has mentioned the call to me. Do they think if they ignore the situation it will just go away?

I know what I thought when I overheard their conversation, which I couldn't help but do, since the argument traveled from the living room to the den to my father's office to upstairs and back down again. I thought that if they believed in me, it wouldn't matter what people said or wondered. I thought that there was only one thing I could do to end this miserable situation, and that was to prove my own innocence. If I didn't have Kelly to help me, I'd have to flounder around by myself.

My mother is happily flustered to see me with a boy—any boy. She clasps Kelly's right hand in both of hers, and smiles as though she had cornered the toothpaste market.

My father talks to Kelly for a few minutes and, thank goodness, stays away from religion. He used to ask my friends if they had been saved, but he stopped when Mary Kay, who never stops talking unless her mouth is full, answered his question with a half-hour recital of how she was saved all right, when the Coast Guard pulled her out of the Gulf of Mexico after her surfboard got carried out on a fast riptide. He dropped the question after that ordeal. I've always had a warm spot in my heart for Mary Kay, who will never know what she did for me.

After they leave, we talk about the kidnapping, keeping our voices low. It doesn't add up to much, just random thoughts. Kelly says he wants to know as much as he can, so I talk and talk and answer his questions.

Finally Della comes in to take the plates. She looks at Kelly suspiciously. "We got fudge brownies. You want dessert now or later?" she asks me.

"How about both now and later?" Kelly asks hopefully.

I suppose it takes an awful lot of food to feed someone as tall as Kelly. "Why don't we take a plate of brownies into the den?" I suggest. "Then we can eat as many as we want."

"Okay with me," Della says. "Come on out to the kitchen, Christina, and I'll fix up a plate for you."

I follow her out to the kitchen, and she turns to me. In a stage whisper that would do credit to Ethel Merman, she says, "What's that boy doing here? Where'd you meet him?"

"What difference does it make? My parents didn't even ask me that."

"It's just that I gotta leave early tonight,"

Della says. "I don't want to leave you alone in the house with just anybody."

"Honestly, Della." I sigh. "You are living in the past. What could happen to me just because I'm alone in the house with a boy?"

"How many possibilities you want?"

"Come off it. You aren't my mother." My words are cross, so I smile to soften them. "It's okay. You can leave early if you want to. Kelly is here just to help me work out something."

"What something?"

"What makes you so curious all of a sudden?"

Della looks at me for a moment, then says, "Oh, never mind. If you say it's okay to go, then I'll go. I don't want to miss the seven o'clock bus."

She puts the brownies on a plate, and I take them, heading back to the dining room to meet Kelly. I have the nagging feeling that Della wasn't concerned just about my being alone in the house with a stranger. She could easily have overheard some of our conversation. Did we say anything that would concern her?

The thought goes out of my head when I

discover that Kelly isn't in the dining room. I go hunting for him and find him already in the den. He is at the glass case, looking at my mother's collection of music boxes.

"There's some good stuff here," Kelly says. "Valuable stuff."

"I suppose so." I put the plate down on the table near the sofa and sit down. "Want to get started? We can get some Cokes later."

Kelly turns and looks at me. "Have you got any paper, and a pen?"

"For what?"

"We want to get things down on paper. It sometimes helps. It's easier to get them into perspective. At least, it always works that way for me."

"On all your kidnapping cases?"

Kelly flops down beside me and grins. "It's a big jump from term papers to solving a kidnapping."

"I'm glad you're going to try. You don't know how much I need your help."

"So here I am," Kelly says. "Get some paper and find out where Della is. We don't want her to listen in."

I get a notebook and come back. Kelly has made great inroads in the brownies.

"Della's busy in the kitchen," I say. "She can't hear us."

"This third person," Kelly says. "For starters, let's list all the things he had to be involved in where you're concerned."

"You keep saying 'he.' Why?"

Kelly shrugs. "I don't know. I guess it's force of habit. You think it's a 'she'?"

"I don't know. I haven't really begun to think about him—her—it. Kelly, we haven't even started, and I'm already confused."

"Stay cool," Kelly says. "We'll work with 'he' until we find out different."

"So we start with a list?"

"Right."

"Better write down 'the gun.' Someone stole it from my father's desk."

"You said it was Loretta."

"But I didn't see Loretta. Della saw the woman, not me. She'd be the only one who could identify Loretta as the person who came to the door."

"Has she done this?"

"I haven't asked her, and no one's questioned anyone in the house since I've come back home."

"Loretta's picture was in the newspaper. So was Zack's. And they were on TV. Didn't Della say anything about seeing the pictures and recognizing the woman?"

"Not to me."

"That's strange. Even if the woman who came to the house wasn't Loretta, I'd think that Della would tell you that."

"You want me to call her in here and ask her?"

"Later," he says. "Let's work on the list for now. What's point two?"

"My clothes. Someone packed a suitcase and got my clothes over to Zack's house."

"Someone who had easy access to your house?"

"How should I know?"

"Okay, okay." He frowns as he writes. "Next point?"

"The typewritten note to Cristabel. Detective York said it was typed on my own portable typewriter."

"Where is the typewriter?"

"They found it in Zack's house. I suppose my father will go down to the police station and get it back, and my suitcase, too. Or maybe he has already. I haven't been upstairs to look."

Della calls from the next room, "Christina, you want to come in here a minute? There's things I need to tell you before I leave."

I look at Kelly, and he nods agreement. "Della," I call back to her, "could you please come in here for a minute?"

She appears in the doorway, slowly, reluctantly. "What for?"

Kelly smiles up at her. "Della, you've seen the news stories about Christina in the paper and on television, haven't you?"

"Yeah."

"So you've seen pictures of Loretta and Zack."

"What about them?"

"We need to know if Loretta is the woman who came to the house the day Christina found the tape on the door."

"I told everybody I never did see that tape on the door."

He shakes his head impatiently. "It doesn't

matter about the tape. We just need to know if you recognized Loretta. Was she the woman you said came to the door that day?"

Della's forehead wrinkles like dried prunes. "I don't know," she says. "All those ladies who come to the door with Avon and *Watchtower* and all that—they all look alike to me, 'cause I don't pay that much attention to them."

"Could you think harder about it and try to remember?"

Her eyebrows wag up and down like warning flags. "No, I couldn't. I don't know who I was talking to that day, and that's all I can tell you."

"But if…"

"What's more," she says to Kelly, "you ain't no policeman who's asking questions for a reason, and I got to go or I'll miss my bus. Christina, you want to come in here for a minute while I tell you something?"

She doesn't wait for an answer, but just leaves the room. I shrug apologetically to Kelly and follow her. Della leads me all the way to the back door before she turns and frowns at me. "I know what the two of you are up to, and it's not good," she says. "You can't go playing policeman and not get hurt."

"You heard our conversation?"

"I heard what you said about thinking there's a third person in all of this. And I'm saying to you to let it lie. Who's this boy think he is, coming in here and getting you started on some foolish chase?"

"He's trying to help me, Della."

"Help you what? Get killed?"

It dawns on me. "Della, you believe what I told everyone about the kidnapping, don't you?"

"It's not my place to believe or not believe. I just know that if you are telling the truth, and those people find out that you're looking for them, you could cause yourself a lot more trouble than you're in right now!"

"I have to prove I wasn't stealing from my grandmother."

"You don't have to prove nothing. People will forget what happened."

"I'll never forget," I tell her, and she stares at me for a few moments, searching deeply into my eyes.

"Okay," she says. "Do it your way. Just don't say I didn't warn you."

"We need to keep this quiet, Della. You won't...well...tell other people?"

She just shakes her head and goes out the back door. She pauses long enough to add, "By the way, somebody from the police brought your typewriter and clothes back. They're up in your room." The door closes and locks behind her.

I return to Kelly.

"Sit down," Kelly says. "I've put on the list the money divided into halves, and Zack and Loretta's conversation that made you think there was a third person involved. What else?"

I work at it a minute, turning it all over and over in my mind in great snatches and scenes. "I think that's it. Should we go into the missing latch or the clean sheets or my fingerprints on the basement heater?"

"Not yet. They'd add up to zilch in the way of evidence, and right now we need to concentrate on the third-person angle."

I realize that we haven't drawn the drapes across the wide windows that overlook the backyard. A sheet of blackness that reflects the interior of the den is all I can see as I look through the windows, but I shudder. It's as though unseen eyes were peering through at me. Quickly I yank on the cords and pull the drapes shut, wrapping a woven cotton wall of security around myself.

"Sit down," Kelly tells me. "Have a brownie. There are a couple left."

His words break the mood of fear, and I join him on the sofa.

"It's pretty obvious that this third person had access to your house," he says. "Who can get in and out easily besides your parents?"

"You think someone burglarized the house?"

"Could be, but I don't know. I'm working on this angle now."

"Well, there's Della, of course, and Rosella."

"Who's Rosella?"

"My father's secretary. He works at home, and she has a little office here, too."

"Does she have a key?"

"Yes."

"Is she the only one outside your family who has a key?"

"Not exactly. My grandmother has a key.

She bought this house for my parents and kept a key for herself."

"Why?"

I look at him for a moment. "Don't ask questions I can't answer." For some reason I'm embarrassed. "Listen, Kelly, we can work on this project without getting into my family relationships, can't we?"

"Okay," he says. "But it is important news that your grandmother has a key."

"But she's family."

He shrugs. "What would happen if her company was having financial problems, and she could explain away a loss with money going to some kidnappers?"

"Kelly! What a rotten thing to say! Cut that out!"

"Do you want to find the answers, or don't you?"

"But my family..."

"I'm not saying your family is involved. We just have to look at this from every direction. Thinking about your grandmother as the third person may lead us to another clue that points to the real person. Understand?"

"I suppose so, but I don't like it much."

"What about someone who works for your grandmother? Would anyone else have a key?"

"No."

"Could anybody get hold of your grandmother's key?"

"Kelly!"

He leans back and smiles at me. "Don't get so shook up. I'm trying to help."

"I know. It's just that this questioning has me all mixed up inside."

"Then let's go to Della. Does she have a key?"

"Yes and no. That is, she doesn't take one home with her, but she knows where the spare key is kept, so if she gets here and no one is home, she can let herself in."

Kelly sits up and whistles. "You've got to be kidding! A house like this, and you have a spare key somewhere, so that anyone can let himself in?"

"Della's the only one outside our family who knows where it is."

"Is it a place where anyone could find it?"

"No. It's in a hidden place on top of the door frame that leads from the garage."

"Does the gardener know this? Anyone like that?"

"No."

"Tell me about Della." He reaches over and eats the last two brownies as I talk.

"She's a nice person."

"You've got to do better than that. What is she like? Does she hang out in bars? Have any vices?"

I giggle. "She's a great dancer, from what she tells me. She likes to live it up on weekends. And she gambles a little."

"This kidnapping was a gamble."

"Oh, come on, Kelly. Della's not the type."

"Let's get to your father's secretary then."

"Rosella? She's not the type either."

Kelly stands up and stretches, then walks to the fireplace and back. He shakes his head at me. "Just who do you think is the type, Christina? Somebody out of an Alfred Hitchcock movie? We're talking about possibilities. Be logical."

"Okay," I say quickly. I can tell that Kelly is

exasperated with me, and I don't want him to be. "Rosella Marsh is a quiet, mousy person who keeps everything inside herself. She has worked for my father for years, and I still don't know what she's really like or what she thinks."

"What kind of work does she do for your father?"

"She does all the important stuff. She researches for him and even writes speeches. He gets all the credit, and she does all the work."

"That's hard to take. Does he pay her enough to make it worthwhile?"

The question surprises me. "I really don't know. I haven't given it any thought."

"She knew your father had a gun in his desk?"

"Everybody knew." His questions are making me terribly uncomfortable. I wish circumstances were different. I wish Kelly and I were talking about things people talk about on dates. I wish...

His voice breaks into my thoughts. "Can you get me Rosella's and Della's addresses? Then I'll start the legwork."

"What legwork?" I stand and face him.

"I'll try to track down anything I can about them or their families. My connection with the TV station might help," Kelly says.

"Their families? One of Della's sons was in jail once."

"Christina, how come you didn't tell me this with the other stuff? Didn't you think it was important?"

"I just didn't think about it, period."

"You have to think. Go over everything in your mind before you go to sleep tonight. Think about anyone else who might have had access to your house without making people suspicious. Think about anyone who could have a motive. Anyone who could reasonably have left town without arousing suspicion. Anyone who..."

"Rosella," I murmur.

He stops. "Rosella what?"

"She was going to visit her parents in Chicago. She had a ticket to fly out of here Monday. She stayed because she was worried about me, she said."

Kelly gives a long, drawn-out sigh. "For real, Christina! How are we going to get anywhere on this investigation? Don't you know that's important, too?"

"I'm trying," I tell him. "This is hard for me. I'm the kind of person who likes to keep things inside. I'm not used to talking to people about how I feel, or probing to see how they feel."

"That's no good," he says. "Psychology one-oh-one. You've got to learn to come out of yourself or you'll end up with ulcers and migraines and all that junk."

"I can't just change the way I am."

"Sure you can. People ought to be able to change when they have to. People can keep changing all their lives."

"But…"

"You're changing right now. Pay attention to yourself. You aren't the same person now that you were last week at this time, are you?"

"I—I guess not."

"And you won't be the same person by the time we're through with our investigation."

I have to think about this a moment. I can't understand the person I used to be. How can I make peace with whatever I'm changing into? I'm getting a headache.

"I'll be going now, but I'll keep in touch," Kelly says.

"When will you call me?"

"When I find something out." He quickly writes some numbers on a scrap of paper and shoves it into my hand. "This is my phone number at home," he says. "Call me if you think of anything else, or if you need me."

I melt when he adds that last bit. He can't imagine how much I needed him, and how I was waiting until he came around.

"What should I do?" I ask.

"We'll just take this one step at a time. Wait until I find out as much as I can. Then we'll move on what comes next." He looks at me solemnly. "And please keep this as quiet as you can. It'll be better if your parents don't know about it either."

I nod. "Thanks, Kelly, for your help." I walk with him to the front door, see him climb into his car, which is too small for his long legs, and shut the door.

Suddenly I'm very tired. I'd like to go to bed, but it's not very late, and I've got homework to catch up on. All the daily trivia have to be replaced in my world—no matter that my life has been torn apart and put back together with some of the pieces missing. The routine goes on.

I take a bath, then prop up a couple of pillows in bed, climbing in with my notebook and my English assignment. It doesn't take long to get into it. The sooner I finish the better, so I plow away.

I am answering a question no one really cares about when I realize that I'm not alone in the house. Maybe there was the click of a doorknob downstairs. If there was, I didn't notice it. I hold my breath and listen as I become aware that softly, very softly, through the thick plush carpeting on the stairway, footsteps are padding, patting, like little slaps with a powder puff. And they are coming up the stairs!

I slip out of bed and grab the bed lamp, tugging the cord from the wall socket. Holding it high, I move toward the doorway, standing to one side, behind the door, which is wide open. I wait.

There are little rustling movements as the person comes closer. I lift the lamp higher.

I can hear the person breathing in the

open doorway of my room. One more step and then...

A soft voice...one I recognize. "Christina?"

Slowly the lamp comes down. My hands are shaking. I am trembling.

"Rosella." I sigh.

She gives a little squeal of fright and peers around the door. "What are you doing?"

"Getting ready to hit you over the head with this lamp," I tell her.

She squeals again, and I quickly add, "I didn't know who was coming up the stairs and into my room! How did I know it was you? I was trying to protect myself." I flip the wall switch that turns on the overhead light.

"I had to come here to bring some papers." She blushes. "I guess I really didn't have to come by. I could have brought them when I came to work in the morning. I really came to see you."

"Me? Why?"

"I've been concerned about you, Christina. I wanted to tell you that I'm sorry for all you've been through."

I motion her into the room and toward my

desk chair. "Sit down, Rosella." I perch on the bed, sitting cross-legged.

"Would you like to talk about it?" she asks me.

I hesitate. "Not really. I've talked about it so much I'm tired of the whole story. Besides, what good would it do when you wouldn't believe me?"

"Maybe I would believe you," she says. "I don't like that Zack. I don't think you'd get mixed up with him."

"What do you know about Zack?" Why do I feel so uncomfortable talking to Rosella? There is something funny here. Rosella has never sought me out for a conversation. The two of us just come and go in the household, never noticing each other as anything more than human beings who inhabit the same planet.

She seems acutely embarrassed now. "I don't want you to misunderstand, Christina," she says. "I wasn't trying to spy on you. It's just that your mother asked me a couple of months ago to investigate that hamburger place that you and Lorna go to every Friday. She wanted to be sure it was…well…acceptable."

I groan. "How well did you get to know Zack Tigus?"

"I didn't get to know him," she answers quickly. "I just visited the place a couple of times and checked it out for cleanliness and… uh…undesirables."

"Undesirables!"

"Well, your mother wanted to protect you."

I flop back on the bed and stare up at the canopy. My mother had Rosella follow me around to make sure I was in good company? The thought angers me. I'm trying to grow up, to become independent! And she checks out a stupid old hamburger place!

Rosella gets up and comes to sit next to me on the bed. She tentatively reaches out and pats my hand, then withdraws hers as though my hand had been a prickly cactus. "Don't be upset with your mother, Christina."

"How overprotective can a mother get?"

There is silence for a moment, and I glance at Rosella. She is staring at the far wall, as though she were looking a thousand miles away. Then she speaks. "I know how you feel. My parents were overprotective, too. They worried incessantly about whom I was going out with, who my friends were. It got so difficult to take that I simply stopped seeing many people. I guess I took the coward's way out."

"You're not a coward."

"I was. Maybe if I'd had the courage to do things on my own, to let them know—politely, of course—that I had to make my own decisions, I'd have had a different life."

"What kind of life?"

She pauses again. Her voice is low as she says, "I would like to have had a job that paid more money. I would like to have been married."

We sit there quietly. I don't know what to say to Rosella. I don't think she knows what to say to me. In all these years I've known her, this is the closest we have ever been, and yet our very closeness leads to miserable embarrassment for both of us.

I try to smooth the situation. "How is your mother?"

"Oh," Rosella says, coming back to reality. "She's fine."

I'm puzzled. Carefully, I prop myself into a sitting position, slide off my bed, and stand up, stretching. Something here is all wrong!

Carefully, I say, "Rosella, I thought your mother was sick."

She looks at me, eyes blinking again. "Oh," she says. "She was, but she's better now."

"That's nice."

"Yes."

"Well," I say, "I do appreciate your coming by to see me, and I know you probably have a million things to do."

She stands, too. "You don't want to talk about it?"

"I'd rather not."

"When you came home, you said something about a third person involved in the kidnapping. I wanted to ask you why you said that."

There is a funny lump in my throat. It's hard to breathe around it. As I talk, my voice is strained and sounds peculiar to my ears. "Detective York said the case was dropped," I tell her. "We'd better leave it that way. Besides, no one believes me."

"I—I think I could believe you. I've never known you to lie, Christina. And I think you're a fine person. You wouldn't try to take your grandmother's money."

"Thanks." I move toward the door.

"That's why I thought…this third person…well…"

She doesn't finish the statement, and I can't. We stand in the room, staring at each other.

I have to break the silence. It's pressing against my head, and I can't bear it. "Well," I repeat. "It was nice of you to come by, Rosella."

She smiles now, a tentative, flickering smile. I can smell the perfume she's wearing as she passes me in the doorway. It's a wild, tropical perfume, and it surprises me. She seems more the rose-garden type. Who is this person called Rosella Marsh? I tell myself the third person couldn't possibly be Rosella! It couldn't! But a flick of suspicion refuses to go away.

I walk with her down the stairway, thinking with each step that it's a long way over the banister to the white marble floor below. I clutch the banister railing with all my strength.

She pauses at the door to smile at me again, and I try to smile back. The minute she's outside, I turn the dead bolt on the front door. Then I check the back door, the side door, and the glass doors that lead into the patio. I have to make sure they are locked tightly. I have to fight back the desperate feeling that I should check them all again. I turn on more lights downstairs and pick a chair with its back to the wall. I am going to wait here until my parents return. I wish I had enough courage to go out to the garage and get the extra key, but I haven't. My God! Even Kelly knows where the key is!

I have never felt so terribly alone—not even in that basement. There, I could see where the danger was coming from. Here, the terror of someone unknown is a hundred times more frightening. This danger has invisible fingers that creep around my throat and squeeze my breath away and make my heart bang against my ribs and make my legs weak when I try to walk.

I want to scream to that unknown someone, "I am afraid of you! I am terrified of you! But I won't give up! Get out of my way, because I won't give up!"

[TEN]

I CAN'T TELL my parents I'm afraid of Rosella. They come in the door, frozen in motion like startled squirrels as they see me sitting near the door to the living room.

I yawn and tell them I was too interested in my book to go to sleep, but I know that my sagging eyelids, heavy with exhaustion, give me away. My mother accepts the words, but her eyes speak to mine.

Like a small child, now that my parents are home, I go to bed and fall asleep immediately. Do I dream of Kelly? Not tonight. Tonight my sleep erases my dreams.

Usually I am alone at the breakfast table, but this morning Della is there, bustling back and forth from the kitchen to the breakfast room like a busy freighter.

"Why are you here so early?" I ask, shaking my napkin out of its carved wooden ring and into my lap.

Della stands before me, her hands folded over the shelf of her rounded belly. "I need to talk to you, Christina."

"About what?" I am cautious, suspicious. Am I always going to feel like this in response to a simple statement? I hope not. It's not the way I want to be.

"About how you should pay attention to what people have been telling you and mind what they say."

"Sit down, Della." I sigh. "I know this is going to be more than a two-minute conversation, and it makes me uncomfortable to have you standing while I sit."

"It's not proper."

"We make our own rules. Please sit down."

She lowers herself into a chair and stares intently at me once more. "What I need to tell you is that the police detective who was here told you to just go about your business and try not to meddle; and your mother and father told you that your grandmother wanted well enough let alone."

"So?"

"So, I'm telling you that I gave a lot of thought to what you and that red-haired, spotted boy were talking…"

"Freckled," I interrupted, wanting to giggle. I wonder how Kelly would like being called "spotted."

She scowls at me and goes on. "Don't matter. What matters is that I know you two are fixing to poke your noses into places they shouldn't be poked."

"Della, Kelly is trying to help me."

She snorts. "Don't tell me that. I don't see that boy as a Good Samaritan. What does he really want? And where'd you meet him, anyway?"

"At…well…Oh, Della, it really isn't any of your business!" I attack my toast ferociously and gulp from my glass of orange juice.

"What you do may not be any of my business, but what I do is my business, and I feel I got to tell you to give up this thing you're doing of trying to play policeman."

"We're not trying to play policemen."

"Christina," she says, bending toward me, "you aren't thinking about how dangerous this could be. You were talking about somebody thinking out this plan and getting those two stupid people to go along with them. Don't you realize that party don't want you to find out who it is? Don't you know you could get hurt?"

I wipe my lips with my napkin and place it beside my plate, deliberately studying Della. "I think you believe me."

"I think you're too smart a girl to go around making up crazy stories, and if what you told us wasn't the truth, it would be one big crazy story."

"Della, I have to get the proof to make everyone believe in me. You know what people believe now."

She shrugs and looks away. "It's just bus gossip. It don't count for anything more than that."

"What's bus gossip?"

"Oh, you know, the things maids talk about on the way to and from work. They're the ones who drag out a story and keep it going. Folks with things on their minds got better to do than that."

"The girls at school believe the newspaper and television stories. So do the teachers."

"They'll forget about it the minute something more interesting comes along. Wait till they find out that blond girl in your class—you know the tall one with those great big glasses—is pregnant. They'll forget all about you."

"What? You don't mean Gloria?"

"Yeah, I do mean Gloria, with those big glasses."

"How do you know that, Della?"

"The girl who works at their house told us on the bus." She smiles at me. "Now, see what I gave you—a good story to spread around until they all forget about what happened to you."

"I can't do that!"

She stands, pressing so hard against the table that it seems to bend. "It's a lot better way of heading than the way you're going, with this trying to be a policeman stuff. That was a bad thing, your being kept in the cold basement of that woman's old rent house the way you say. Don't you want to forget it?"

"I want to do what I think best." I stand, too, and look at my watch. "I've got to hurry, or I'll be late for school."

"Go on then," she says. Her voice changes, softens. "But, please, Christina, think about what I told you."

"I'll think about it, but I'm not going to change my mind."

"You and your grandmother, most stubborn people I ever seen."

I take a sharp breath. It hurts. "I am not like my grandmother," I say slowly, deliberately.

"Not just like her," she answers quickly, "but those times she's been here I see there's a lot of her in you—the stubborn part and some good parts, too."

I don't answer. I do all the last-minute things, scoop up my books, and run to my car. On the way I remove the extra key from the door frame and drop it in my bag. At the end of the drive, instead of turning right, I turn left. What am I doing?

A feeling inside me tells me that in spite of what Kelly has told me, in spite of what I know I should do, I am not going to school this morning. I'm driving to the Tigus house. There's something I've got to do.

What? I search for the answer, but there is

only silence. Maybe the answer will come later. I hope so.

At the first shopping center I pull into a parking slot, go into the drugstore, and phone the school. I tell the office attendant I won't be in today.

She immediately says what she probably says to anyone who phones in an absence, "Oh, dear. I do hope you'll feel much better tomorrow."

I didn't tell her I was sick, but I don't feel like explaining. It was her idea, not mine. I let it drop and hang up the receiver.

There's a doughnut place next door. I don't really want anything to eat, but I have to kill some time. I want to talk to Loretta, not to Zack, and he will probably still be at his house. The doughnut tastes dry and crumbly and gaggingly sweet, but the coffee is good and hot. I sip at it until I notice the counter girl glaring at me and two customers waiting for stools. I put down my change and leave quickly, embarrassed at listening so hard for inner messages that I'm unaware of what is happening around me.

So that hidden part of my mind has told

me to talk to Loretta. That's what I'll do. I remember the address of the house from newspaper stories. I know how to get there.

As I drive, an uncomfortable thought nags at me, but I can't put my finger on it. Something Della said…there was something that wasn't right—out of focus. Was it my suspicion about why Della should want me to stop looking for this third person? Why should she care? I can't believe gossip on the bus bothers her. And I really don't think she's that concerned with this "danger" she talked about. Why can't people just let me alone and let me do what has to be done? I'm glad I have Kelly on my side. How could I accomplish anything without Kelly?

The morning rush of traffic is long over, so it doesn't take much time to drive to the part of the city where the old Tigus house squats on a tattered lawn. The house needs paint, its rust red trim faded and peeling in little curls. The upstairs windows, with their crooked, slanted window shades, give a cross-eyed stare down the pointed nose of the front porch. I park down the street, where I can watch the house without being seen.

There is a car in the driveway. Zack probably drives it to work, and he hasn't left yet. Is he still working at that hamburger place? It occurs to me that I don't know, that I really know very little about what I'm doing. Maybe I should wait and talk to Kelly. No, the compulsion is strong. I sit in the car, twisting my keys over and over in my cold fingers, waiting.

The emotions I feel as I look at this house, where I was kept prisoner, are so strong and so conflicting that I feel sick to my stomach and have to fight back waves of nausea. Down in that basement it was like being buried, and the house is the gravestone.

I close my eyes for a moment, gripping the keys so tightly they dig painfully into my fingers. When I open my eyes, I see Zack getting into his car. He is alone. He pulls the car out of the driveway, backs with a gunning of the motor and a cloud of thick gray exhaust, and speeds off in the opposite direction from where I am sitting, watching him. Good.

I put my keys back into the ignition and drive to a spot directly in front of the Tigus house. A window curtain flutters and is still. Loretta is inside, and she has seen me drive up. Strange Loretta with her nervous dedication to Zack and her ironing board...Loretta, the weakest link in the chain.

I am getting out of the car when this thought hits me. Of course! Now I know why my subconscious mind sent me here. Loretta is the weakest. I know about Zack, who is all loud bluster. I don't know about the third member of this trio, but I have to assume that he—or she—has more going for him than Loretta does. Loretta is the weakest link, and I am here to see if the weakest link might break.

I walk up the steps and ring the bell. No one answers, but I can sense Loretta's presence on the other side of the door, the way a fox feels out the presence of a rabbit down his hole.

"Open the door," I say loudly, "or I will stand here and scream bloody murder until your neighbors send for the police!"

The door opens a crack. I push it open, then walk inside and close the door behind me.

"Why'd you want to come here?" Loretta is sullen.

"I didn't," I tell her. "I don't like being here at all. I came because I have to talk to you."

"About what?"

"Go into the den and we'll sit down. I don't want to stand here and talk." I find that I have taken command and Loretta is obeying me, somewhat reluctantly.

"I got to finish my ironing," she says.

I shiver as the chill of the house penetrates my blazer. Carefully I perch on the edge of one of the chairs in the den.

Loretta, following my example, sits on another chair, her arms folded across her chest as though she were hugging herself.

"What do you want?" she asks.

"I want you to give me some answers to questions I have."

"Zack told me I wasn't supposed to say nothing to nobody."

"Not even when your life is in danger?"

Her eyes grow wider. "What are you talking about? In danger from what?"

"Not from what...from whom. From that person who thought up this scheme."

"You aren't making sense. What person are you talking about? You don't even know." She attempts a sneer and brushes back a thin strand of hair, but her eyes drop.

"You're right. I don't know who this person

is. I just know that someone else is involved. I came to ask you to tell me who it is."

"You're crazy!"

"No, you are, because you haven't thought ahead. If this person ever gets afraid that you'd tell his identity, then what do you think will happen to you?"

She jumps in her chair. "To me? Why not to you? You're the one nosin' around."

"I'm in danger, too," I say.

"Are you talking about him killing us?"

"It could happen."

"You, sitting there so cool. You aren't scared?"

"Of course I'm scared! That's why I want to find out who this person is. Right now he thinks he's safe, that everyone has bought the story of the extortion that I'm supposed to have masterminded. But one of these days he's going to get nervous—maybe even if I let the investigation drop. Each day the thought is going to creep up on him that someone might find out, that he could be caught. I don't know who he is, so I don't think he'll be so concerned about me. But you know, and he'll be afraid that you'll talk. And some night, when it's so dark that the neighbors can't see, and Zack is kept late at the hamburger place, and no one will know…then he'll come creeping around this house and peering in the windows until he finds you, and he'll…"

"Stop that!" Loretta shrieks and jumps from her chair.

I jump up, too, and grab her shoulders. "I'm not making things up, Loretta. That's just the way he'd think!"

She shakes herself free of my grip, turns, and bursts into tears. "Go away," she says. "I can't tell you anything! I gotta talk to Zack."

I try to reason with her, but the mood has been broken. Like an old record with a scratched groove she keeps saying, "I gotta talk to Zack."

Maybe Loretta is more afraid of Zack than of this person.

So I walk to the front door, Loretta on my heels, eager to shut and bolt the door behind me.

"I'm going to find out who he is," I tell her.

Her gaze is defiant. "You think so? Well, there's a lot you don't know!"

"What makes you think so?"

"I know so."

"Is it because I'm saying 'he' instead of 'she'?"

She blinks and stares, then says, "Go on... get out of my house!"

I walk to my car, wondering. Has she given away something? I can't tell. I don't know. I'm not going to give up on Loretta. I'm going to work on this weakest link until it breaks open with the information I need. I just hope I can do it before the third person finds out what I'm up to. If I just had an inkling of who it could be—some idea to work on. My guess is Rosella...underpaid, frustrated, in a miserable little job where her boss gets all the credit for the work she does...where she can't meet people, where she becomes more and more unhappy until...Is that Rosella? Is that how she thinks? I barely know who she is. In the daylight she is much less threatening than she was in the quiet of the house last night.

The perfume she wears...maybe inside she's itching to dash off to South America and live as abandoned a life as she can work up on the spur of the moment—with Cristabel's money. The image of Rosella as a femme fatale makes me want to laugh.

I start the car, with a last look at the house I hate, and at the woman, who flips back from the peephole she's made in the edge of the front-window curtain as she sees me glance that way. Where to now? Maybe I should call Kelly and ask what the next step should be. But Kelly will be in class, and that's where he told me to be. I can't go back to school yet. Right now the routine of classes is so far from my world that if I had to sit through them I would scream with frustration and probably scare Madame DeJon into fits.

Aimlessly, I drive to the parking lot next to the hamburger place, cautiously dipping into and out of a pothole as I work my way through the pits and lumps of the paving to a spot where I can see inside.

Zack's not open for business yet, but he's inside, lazily getting things ready. I watch him pour hot water into a large coffee urn. He wipes his hands on his already stained pants, then yawns widely and scratches his chest and under his armpits. Does he own this place?

Lease it? Why was he ready to walk away and leave it? I've seen a couple of helpers there with him. Did they take over while I was living in the basement of the Tigus house?

I used to laugh at the little light bulbs that appeared over people's heads in comic strips when they got brilliant ideas. I don't laugh now. An idea strikes me, and it's very much like a light turning on. I know the next step. I know what to do! I'm delighted with myself for getting it together.

I start the ignition, and for the first time catch Zack's attention. He stares at the car and at me, his mouth slightly open, his lower jaw limp. He resembles a catfish giving its last gasp.

Ignoring him, I ease the car out into the traffic of the access road, pull into the freeway, and head toward the police station downtown.

My arrival there is very different today from the way it was when I was quickly escorted through the back door by Detective York. Today I walk up the front steps and to the information booth in the tiny lobby, where an elderly man in uniform is scanning the morning paper and rubbing his left ear.

"Where can I go to look up records?" I ask him.

He stares at me curiously for an instant. "Depends on what kind of records."

"Whether or not someone has been in jail and when. And if someone owns property or is renting. That sort of thing."

"Whoa!" he answers. "You've got a couple of places all lumped together. Aren't even in the same building."

"Well, could you tell me where these places are and how I can get there?"

He stares at me, but as I stare back trying to discover his thoughts, he shuts them off and his eyes become little pools of cold coffee. "Tell you what," he says. "I'll get someone down here who can lend you a hand."

"I can do this myself."

"Pretty complicated business." He waves toward a chair—another of those awful green plastic-and-chrome things. "You just sit there a couple minutes. He'll be right down."

"Who will?"

But he busies himself with a phone, turning away from me. I seem to have no choice, so I perch on the chair, ankles and knees tucked together, waiting for whoever it is to come and help me.

I watch the elevator doors open and shut, swallowing assorted flavors of humanity and spitting out others. Then I see a face I recognize—Detective Jason York. He comes directly toward me, and I stand up to meet him.

"Want to talk to me?" he asks.

"I didn't come for that," I say. "I came to look up some records. I need information that wasn't in the news stories."

"I know. I was called and told you were here." He waves a thumb toward the officer in the information booth.

"But..." I grip my hands together, so frustrated I want to cry out. "All I came to do was check out some things."

"Okay," he says. "Come on upstairs and we'll talk it over."

"You mean you'll help me do this?"

"That's what we're here for."

Now I can smile at him. I follow him into the gaping elevator for the ride to the third-floor offices of the Homicide Division.

We go into the interrogation room we were in before, and I shiver as I sit in the same chair.

He is watching me shrewdly. "Brings back some unpleasant memories, doesn't it?"

I nod, and he adds, "You'll get over it. No matter what comes along to cut us up, eventually we get over it. How come you aren't in school today?"

"I can't go back until I find out some things," I say.

"Uh-huh. Answers you think you'll find in records." I lean forward eagerly, pushing away the large stinking ashtray filled with stale butts that's under my nose. "Something bothers me. If Zack and Loretta own that hamburger stand and the house they live in, then why would they just walk away and leave them? The property would be worth enough so that it doesn't make sense to give up. But they were planning to leave town."

"I'll pull a couple of files, and we'll see what we can come up with." He's gone for a little while, and I push the ashtray all the way over to the wall.

When he returns, he sits at the desk going through some papers in the manila folder he has brought with him. He reads intently, picking at a little red spot that is beginning to swell on his chin. Finally he looks up. "You gave me an easy one to answer. When Zack and Loretta were in the ID department, they volunteered some information as the forms were filled out. Zack Tigus stated that he was managing a hamburger stand on a lease. The lease is due to run out at the end of the month, and the rent will be raised. Loretta said she had inherited the house, but a large corporation has bought a four-block area from the owners of those old houses to develop as another shopping area. The houses have been leased back to the owners at a low rent until it comes time to tear them down."

"So it wouldn't have bothered them at all to leave the country and the business and the house."

"Doesn't look as though it would."

I sigh. Things are shaping up, coming together. So far, so good. "I had to know that," I say. "Thanks."

"How about the rest of what you wanted?"

"The information office told you what I asked?"

"About jail records? Yeah."

I lean back in my chair. The plastic is hard

against my back. "I'm trying to track down an area. Could we check out some names? I'd like to know more about Zack's jail record and the people he knew in jail. I'd like to find out if Loretta was ever in jail."

He raises one eyebrow, but simply says, "Remember that I told you the tracking comes from my department."

"I know, but Kelly said…"

"Kelly?"

"He's a…a friend. He believes my story. He's probably the only one who really does, and he's the only one who said he'd help me."

"I said I'd help you."

"But that's different. You also said you had a lot of other cases to work on."

"That's right." He stretches back in his chair, locking his hands behind his head. "Three murders last night, for instance. One of them a bar brawl, where no one, including the bartender, was sober enough to know what happened or who fired the gun. The other two were random killings—very little in the way of leads. And we've got some old murders to work on, and assorted robberies and burglaries and…" He shakes his head quickly and sits up-right. "Well, enough of all that. I'm still inter-ested in your case."

"But Kelly and I have more time to work on it."

"You and this Kelly, whoever he is, are working out a fantasy. In the world of crime, people have guns without consciences on the trigger ends. They try to take what they want, and they don't let anyone get in their way. If you're a nuisance to them, with your prying around, they could just as easily put an end to you as squash a roach."

He leans toward me, against the desk, and I can see the bulge of a shoulder holster under his coat. For some reason this scares me, and makes his words seem even more real. "I'll get someone in the department to check out the records we need," he says. "I'll get them to you as soon as I can. Will you trust me?"

"Yes."

"Going through records is a good idea. Maybe it will tell us something. Maybe it will jog something in your memory, and you'll come up with a piece of information that will help us move further."

I stand and try to smile at Detective York again. It's a shaky smile, but it's there.

He reaches out a large hand and shakes my shoulder gently. "Hang in there," he says. "Go on with your normal routine—especially, stop playing hooky from school." He moves around the desk. As an afterthought he says, "And tell this little friend of yours—this Kelly—to stop the game right now. Investigating a crime—any crime—is not a job for amateurs."

"You'll call me soon with the information?"

"I'll call. How soon I can't promise."

It's a short walk back through the Homicide Division room and down the hall and into the elevator, with its assortment of talls and shorts and wides and thins, all squeezing against each other, with every thing meeting but eyes.

I'll have to call Kelly and tell him what Detective York said. I don't think Kelly will agree that we should drop our investigation. I hope he won't. Maybe I'm being stubborn, but I've got to carry this through, even if I have to work alone.

[ELEVEN]

I STOP IN a drive-in to get a hamburger and a Coke, then take them to Memorial Park. It's quiet in the park. A couple of women joggers puff by, their faces pink from exertion, their heavy breasts bouncing up and down under their sweatshirts. A squirrel peels itself from the camouflage of a nearby oak tree and scampers to my feet, begging for crumbs. I give him the last chunk of soggy bun and go back to my car. The sky is turning gray, and the pollen from the flowering ligustrum is making my nose itch.

It's not far to a phone booth. I have the scrap of paper with Kelly's phone number on it in my handbag, and I fish for it, banging an elbow on the accordion glass door of the booth. The phone rings and rings, and finally a woman answers it with a tired sound that passes for a "hello."

I ask for T. J. Kelly, and she says, "He's at class."

"Do you know when he'll be home?"

"There's no telling. He goes from class to the studio. If they've got a big story to work on and need his camera, then he sometimes gets home later than usual."

"What's usual?"

There's a pause. "Who is this?"

I can't seem to communicate with this woman. She must be Kelly's mother. Doesn't sound young enough to be one of his sisters. I find I'm hesitant about giving my name, but I can't be. Kelly must call me back. So I tell her.

She doesn't react. "I'll tell him you called," she says. "I'm writing it down on the blackboard we keep by the phone in the kitchen. Kelly usually looks there when he comes home. So do all the kids. They know there's no way to remember all the messages that come in."

"Yes," I murmur.

"You said something else?"

"No."

"I didn't catch it."

Our words interlock and spin into a garble of sound, so that we can't hear one another. I keep quiet to give her a chance, and she says, "Anything else?"

"No. That's it. Thank you very much." I am prim and polite, instead of shouting, "I need Kelly! Tell him it's urgent!" the way I wish I could.

There is a click of the receiver in my ear. There's nothing to do now but wait until Kelly calls—and until Detective York calls. Wait… wait…wait. I can't go back to school. To kill time I go to the library and read all the news stories about what happened. It makes me sick to read them, but I must find out everything I can. Then I go home to wait for Kelly's call.

But Kelly doesn't phone, and he doesn't come by. The ten o'clock newscasters cover two fires by arson, four holdups of savings-and-loan offices, an angry meeting of the school board, and a flash news item about a ten-car pileup on the 610 Loop, with films of the accident to follow. Kelly, will you get home too late to phone me?

The phone rings, and I hurry to answer it, realizing that I'm the only one who would. My mother and father have gone to a bridge party at their club.

"Kelly?" I say eagerly, but there is a long pause. "Hello? Who's there?" I ask. My throat is cold. My hand grips the receiver as though it could never let go. I know I should hang up, but I can't move.

Then it comes…a whisper. "Keep your nose out of things," it says, and it adds a string of obscenities. I can't tell whether the voice belongs to a man or a woman. The whisper disguises it completely. "Do you understand?" it asks.

There is no way I can answer. No way. Like a robot, with jerky, stiff motions, I hang up the receiver, staring at the phone. My stomach hurts. The phone rings again, but I don't answer. Should I call Detective York? Should I call my mother and father and ask them to come home from the club?

Taking a deep breath, I force myself to move away from the phone. I turn off the television set and slowly go up the stairs. I should have known it would be like this. Maybe I'm asking for it. But what choice have I got? I can't go on the other way!

In the bathroom I throw up, and the pain that has gripped my stomach begins to lessen. I put on a nightgown and climb into bed, hugging the covers around my chin. Most of the lights in the house are on. I'll leave them on.

Tomorrow Kelly will call me. I'll have to be patient until tomorrow. The phone doesn't ring again, thank God. Tomorrow, Kelly... tomorrow.

Tomorrow comes and another tomorrow. I don't go to school. I manufacture a sore throat and convince my mother that the light sprinkling of acne under my chin is the beginning of a rash. She keeps me in bed, and runs out to Alfred's kosher restaurant for a quart of chicken soup to go. She read in an article once that Jewish-mother chicken soup was better than penicillin, so when anyone in the family is sick, that's what he gets, although she leaves out the "Jewish mother" part when she feeds the soup to my father.

I'm grateful there are no more whispering late-night phone calls. Could the caller know I'm not home alone?

This is a quandary. I can't stay in bed forever, but I can't go to school. I went to classes that one day, and I managed to get through the day without coming apart in little pieces. But I can't do it again. It takes too much energy, and I want to use that energy to do all the work needed to prove myself. Where is Kelly? I wonder why he hasn't called. I can't call him back. I'd probably find myself talking to his mother again, and I'd feel like a fool.

It's early afternoon, and my bed has become hot and boring and full of lumps I didn't know were there before. So I dress in jeans and an old plaid shirt, then go to the den and sit on the floor cross-legged in front of the television set, watching *Sesame Street* on Channel 8. Lorna comes into the room.

"Hi," she says in a little voice, hanging back in the doorway to the kitchen, ready to jump away as though she thought I would shout "Boo" at her.

I scramble to my feet. "Lorna! I didn't know you were here!"

"Della let me in the back door."

"Well, come in. Sit over here. I'll get us something to eat. Move those cushions out of the way." I'm babbling. This is my best friend. Why am I acting as though she were a stranger?

Lorna sits on the edge of the sofa. "You haven't been at school for three days. They said in the attendance office that you were sick."

"Uh…yes," I say.

She looks at me with a little wrinkle of worry branching her eyebrows. "Are you feeling better now?"

"I think so."

"I've—we've missed you at school."

I flop on the sofa beside her. "Oh, Lorna, I can't go back to Madame DeJon's!"

"You have to! No one can just drop out of school. What about graduation next year? What about college?"

I groan. "I can't even think about next year. It's hard enough to think about tomorrow."

Lorna touches my hand. "Please come back, Chrissie. I'm there to help you. And you needn't mind what others do or say."

"I can't go there and face them, knowing they believe that lie about me."

Her eyes blank over for an instant, and I wonder, with a feeling as though someone had socked me in the stomach, if she's thinking about the gossip and the lie and the people who believe it, or if she still has doubts about me, too.

Lorna makes her voice cheerful and optimistic. I'm sure she's practiced the speech on the way over here, because it comes out in a polished rhythm. "Everything passes, Christina. People may gossip about you today, but there's something new to gossip about tomorrow, and then they'll forget about you."

"They'll never forget. I have to prove that I was telling the truth. Besides, there's no gossip that will be important enough to wipe out the wrong gossip they've got going about me."

She perks up, and her eyes snap. "Oh, no? Wait until I tell you the latest we've found out! Everybody's talking about it!"

"What?"

"Gloria!" Her voice is almost a whisper. "She's pregnant! Can you believe it?"

Suddenly I am filled with such sorrow for Gloria that I want to hold her and weep with her. I feel at one with Gloria, yet I've never really known her well. It doesn't seem to matter. I don't really know myself either.

"What's the problem?" Lorna is peering into my face. "Isn't that exciting news?"

"No," I say. "It's sad news. It breaks my heart."

Lorna looks away, embarrassed. "Come on, Christina. Stop kidding. Don't you want to know what you've missed in class? I brought your homework assignments."

She holds out a sheet of paper, which is covered with her tiny, neat handwriting. "It's a lot to make up."

"I don't mind," I say. "I'll just stay home and make up homework forever and ever."

"I don't understand you," she says. "Are you trying to be funny?"

"I don't feel a bit funny, and I'm having so much trouble understanding myself, I can't expect you to understand me, Lorna."

"But I want to," she says.

"Why?"

"Because I'm your friend."

Maybe I'm becoming overly suspicious. A part of my mind is asking if Lorna would really want to remain my close friend if she had doubts that I had been kidnapped. Who'd want to have an extortionist for a friend? Lorna might. She'd enjoy being a martyr, loyal to the end, especially if it bugged her mother that she was sticking by me.

I shake my head, trying to clear away the thoughts that, like little sharp-toothed rats, are gnawing away chunks of my self-esteem. I take her friendship at face value. After all, haven't we been friends since first grade?

"Let's get some sandwiches," I tell Lorna, holding out my hand to her and tugging her up from the sofa. "I'm starving."

She smiles back eagerly. "And I can go over the homework with you! I've got lots of time. You will come back to school, won't you?"

"Someday," I say, and I laugh, which causes Lorna to laugh, too, the meaning of the answer disappearing in rings of giggles.

We eat and we study, and the afternoon passes. Kelly still hasn't called. I don't understand. I thought he wanted to help me.

In the distance I hear the doorbell ring, but Lorna and I are busy, and I don't pay attention. It's Della's job to take care of interruptions.

But a voice over my left shoulder says, "Hi, Christina!" and I jump and whirl around.

"Kelly! Where have you been?"

He looks puzzled, and I realize that Lorna is staring openmouthed at Kelly and then at me, and back again at Kelly, like a spectator at a tennis match between Eric the Red and Phyllis Diller. I remember my manners.

"Lorna Darvey...T. J. Kelly," I stammer. As an afterword to Lorna I say, "Kelly is...uh... helping me."

"Helping you what?" Lorna asks.

Kelly moves into the room, smiling and narrowly missing the coffee table. He is taking Lorna in carefully. I don't blame him, because Lorna is good-looking—no doubt about it. I feel a tug of jealousy, and for a moment I don't know whether I want to righteously push it away or experience it and enjoy the misery. Kelly's next words distract me.

"I was hoping you'd have a few minutes to answer some questions for me," he says.

"Well, sure. That is...Why didn't you call me back?"

"What are you talking about? Did you call me?"

"I called you Wednesday. I said it was important. Your mother told me she was writing my name on the blackboard by your kitchen phone, and you'd see it there and call me."

Kelly groans and flops into a low chair, his long legs spread out in front of him. "I don't know why she does that to me! She's got this thing about girls calling boys being all wrong, and after that chick in my eco class last year got it into her head to phone twice a day and…" He breaks off. "I told my mom to let me know if you called, Christina, but she gets things mixed up sometimes. Sorry I didn't get your message. We don't even have a black-board by the kitchen phone."

Lorna stands and begins to gather her things together. "I've got to leave," she says. "It's nearly dinnertime, and I'm going with my parents to that Russian collection on exhibit at the art museum." Her eyes are telling me, "Call me as soon as you can and fill me in on this Kelly."

"Okay," I say, giving a double answer. "I'll see you."

"I'll talk to you tomorrow," Lorna says, "and you be at school Monday…you hear?"

I smile, and Lorna makes a few polite re-marks to Kelly, who uncurls himself from the low chair with some difficulty and says all the right things back to her. Lorna insists on going to the door by herself, and in a way I'm glad to see her leave. I want so badly to talk to Kelly.

For a few seconds we sit and look at the walls in silence, until we hear the back door close. Then Kelly and I turn toward each other eagerly, speaking together.

"What have you done?"

"What do you know?"

He backs off first. "Tell me why you called me. What's up?"

"I went to the police station to look up some records."

"What kind of records?" Kelly is interested.

"I thought it would be a good idea to look up Zack's police record, and also to see if any one else we know has any kind of record—anything that could tie him in with Zack."

"What did you find out?"

"Nothing yet. I talked to Detective York. He told me he'd do it for me."

Kelly thinks hard, then says, "When?"

"He didn't make any promises. He said he'd do it when he could."

"Damn!"

"Kelly, he also said that we should stay out of the investigation. He said it could be dangerous since we don't know who we're up against."

Kelly rubs his hands through his hair, leaving wisps standing on end. "Do you go along with this?"

"I wanted to see what you thought."

"But I asked you a question. You didn't answer it."

I sigh. "Oh, Kelly, I want so much to get to the truth in all this. I'm impatient, and I don't want to wait for Detective York to get into it on his free time."

"I'm glad to hear you say that," Kelly says.

"Then you feel that way, too?"

He grins at me. "You know it! We haven't got that much time to fool around with."

His words puzzle me. "Why? What do you mean?"

He shrugs, and his gaze shifts to examine a large painting on the far wall as he answers. "Isn't that what you've told me? Isn't that what we were talking about before? We'd have to find who that third person was, or the trail would get cold? The more time that passes after a crime, the harder it is to discover who did it."

His words make sense, and in a way I am mollified; but something in the back of my mind nags at me. I've had this feeling before. Something isn't quite right, but I don't know what it is. What's the matter with me? Am I going to go through life being suspicious of everyone?

"Do you feel that you'd be in any danger, Christina?" Kelly's face is serious.

"I—I don't know. I don't think so." Why don't I want to tell him about the phone call?

"That's good," he says. He smiles again. "Then we'll get to work."

"Kelly...how about you? Do you think I'll be in danger?"

He laughs. "Not from what we've found out so far!" But he adds, reacting to the expression on my face, "Don't look so upset. We have only three suspects, and I don't think any of them would hurt you."

"Three? Where did we get three?"

We are close together now, voices low,

heads almost meeting. I can smell Kelly's after-shave lotion—a woodsy kind of fragrance that seems to go with his wild red hair. I like it.

"Rosella, Della, and your grandmother."

I gasp. "I told you to forget about that, Kelly! Leave my grandmother out of it! She wouldn't do a thing like that!"

"Wouldn't she?" He fishes some papers out of his shirt pocket and unfolds them, spreading out the creases with his thumb.

"A guy I know on one of the papers got hold of some financial information for me. It seems that your grandmother's company spread itself pretty thin when it began going in for land development as a sideline. They're in kind of a bind in that department, with taxes coming on a lot stronger than sales. And they haven't had such good luck lately with their natural-gas exploration either."

I put a hand on his arm to stop him. "Kelly, it doesn't matter! What kind of woman would have her own granddaughter kidnapped? Not Cristabel, I can promise you!"

"Nobody hurt you, did they? They didn't push you around, and you got fed, and there weren't any other problems. Right?"

"But…"

"If we're going to do this step-by-step, we've got to cover everything, Christina. We can't just go on your emotions. That isn't scientific detecting."

I push back my chair, staring at my outstretched feet. "Then let's forget the whole thing."

"You're kidding!"

"I am not! Either you leave Cristabel out of this, or forget about helping me. Do you understand, Kelly?" I'm glaring at him now.

"Okay," he says, and he gives me another big, lopsided smile. "I didn't know you felt so strongly about it."

I make myself relax. I'm tired. I don't like getting emotional and spilling out all the things inside my head. All I want is a nice peaceful life in which I can find out who I am. I just want to think about me for a while. I wish it weren't impossible.

"Oh, Kelly," I say, "it seems so hopeless. We're going on the possibility that it has to be someone I know—someone who has access to the house and who knows where my clothes are and where my father keeps his gun. What if it's just a very clever person who's good at burglarizing houses?"

"Yeah. It's a possibility all right."

"So what can we do?"

"We can investigate those two, at least. If they don't tie in with Zack, then we'll have to take it from another direction."

A thought comes to me. "Then how about going from Zack's direction right from the first?"

"Like how?"

There are footsteps in the doorway, and my mother sails into the room, floating gauzy sleeves behind her. She looks surprised, pleased, and disturbed all at the same time when she sees Kelly, and it's easy to see what's going on in her mind.

"Kelly, isn't it? How nice," she says, floating toward him.

He manages the trick of unbending again, and reaches down to shake her hand.

My mother looks at me uncertainly. "Did we forget to tell you that Cristabel is coming for dinner tonight?"

"Here?"

"I thought it would be nice. We need to…"

She stops, glancing at Kelly. She obviously doesn't want to fill him in on family business.

"I'd better be going then," Kelly says.

"No," I tell him. I turn to my mother, knowing I am breaking a hard-and-fast rule from early childhood. In front of Kelly I say, forcing my mother's hand, "Please, may Kelly stay for dinner, too?"

It's hard to grit your teeth and smile at the same time, but my socially correct mother manages it nicely. "Why, what a lovely idea. You can stay, can't you, Kelly?"

"Sure," Kelly says.

I give an inward sigh of relief. I counted on the fact that Kelly would avoid reading between the lines. I know he wants to meet Cristabel, and I want to have him there so our family conversation can stay on a nice inane surface level.

"You might change out of your jeans, dear," my mother says. "I'll stay here and chat with Kelly."

So I dash upstairs, take a quick shower, and put on a dress and as much makeup as I can to have something going for me. I come away from the mirror as about a four on a scale of one to ten, which is a lot better than the minus I was before.

Kelly looks at me appreciatively when I re-enter the den, and that's all I need. My morale goes up enough to carry me through dinner, which is a disaster.

Cristabel has made an effort to come, I'm sure, because she must feel as ill at ease with me as I do with her. But she is gracious and self-possessed. She reminds me of Queen Elizabeth at a ceremony of state. She must have the same backbone and nervous system.

My mother is in her role of effervescent and charming hostess, which she plays to perfection. My father is warm dignity in a dull gray suit. I am a dutiful and mostly silent daughter; whereas Kelly is just Kelly. He accidentally sloshes water from his goblet on the tablecloth, and drops his roll on the floor. He flatters Cristabel, and seems to enjoy himself wholeheartedly. No one told Kelly he had a part in this play.

Della serves, throwing little frowns, like darts, in Kelly's direction, but none of them hits the target. I watch the lily bulbs in the bowl in the center of the table. The sprouts are much higher, stronger. They seem to grow under my gaze. Tips of green buds are beginning to show.

Kelly makes the mistake of saying something about people who want to nationalize the oil companies, and Cristabel is off and running, not waiting for Kelly to finish his sentence so she can find out whether he's for or against the idea. For the next twenty minutes she puts on an Academy Award scene that outdoes Angela Lansbury. My father finally breaks in to say that the coffee is getting cold, and wouldn't it be nice to have fresh cups in the living room.

Kelly and I excuse ourselves and wander into the den.

"Your grandmother is an interesting person," Kelly says.

"The word 'interesting' is an understatement."

"Are you like her?" he asks. "I think you are, in a way."

"No!" Why does this question make me so angry? "I'm not a bit like Cristabel!"

"I think you are—oh, not in looks, or anything like that. I mean that I think you've both got a lot of guts."

"Great," I say. "I needed that compliment to make my evening complete."

"Forget it," Kelly says. "I've got to start for home pretty soon. We'd better decide what our next step should be."

"Detective York said he'd get any record information to me as soon as he had it."

"But how about in the meantime? No telling how long that will take."

"What do you want me to do?"

"Talk to Rosella and Della. See if you can get any more information from them. And I've got an idea I'm going to work on for now."

"What idea?"

"I'll tell you about it later."

"Okay," I answer. I have an idea of my own, but if that's the way Kelly wants to be, then I'll keep it to myself. Besides, I'm still mad at him for comparing me to Cristabel. All I want is to be myself.

Kelly leaves. I go into the living room and say good night. It's easy. No one feels like talking to me now. I take my books up to my room, throw them on the chair, and get back into my jeans.

I've got the idea, and now is the time to

put it into practice. I'm going to see if Zack can't lead me to this mystery person—the one who planned the kidnapping so carefully.

It doesn't take long to look up the number of the hamburger place. A woman's voice answers the phone, and over the noise in the background of tinny, piped-in radio music and someone shouting orders for with and without onions, she yells at me that Zack is off duty and not due in until the next morning at eleven. Good. That's what I was hoping for.

The home phone for Zachariah Tigus is listed, too, so I jot it on a slip of paper, make sure I have a couple of quarters in my purse, grab a sweater, and run down the stairs. At the living room I poke my head in, say, "Gotta go out for a couple of minutes," and disappear out the front door before any of them has a chance to ask me where, when, or why.

My Cutlass is in the garage. It takes just a few minutes to pull out onto the street.

I follow the route I know over to Zack's neighborhood. There is a gas station on the nearest main street, and most gas stations have outdoor phone booths in them. This one is no exception. I keep the door open, so no light shows. I can see enough from the bluish arc light on the street corner to dial Zack's number. It's not too late. I'm pretty sure he won't be in bed yet. He'd probably be stretched out in one of those lumpy overstuffed chairs, watching television, while Loretta irons something...anything.

The receiver is sweaty in my hand, and I can only breathe in little, short gasps. I am counting the rings, and on the fifth Zack answers. I am so relieved I find it hard to think. What if it had been Loretta? I don't know what I would have said.

"Hello? Hello?" Zack's voice is impatient.

I whisper. I found out the hard way it makes a great disguise for a voice.

"Meet me," I say.

"What? Is this...?"

I interrupt, trying to put force and power into my whisper. "You know who this is. I want you to meet me. It's important."

"Where?"

"I don't have to tell you that. You know where to find me."

Quickly I hang up, get inside my car on the run, and drive two blocks to Zack's street.

I pull to the curb, down about five houses from his, and turn out my lights. Then I wait.

It doesn't take long. Zack comes out of his front door and climbs into the green car sitting in the driveway. As he backs out, he turns the car in my direction. I barely have time to scoot down on the seat, out of sight, before he passes me.

I make a U-turn, glad there are no cars parked opposite me, turn on my lights, and try to follow Zack around the corner. I didn't realize that cars look so much alike in the dark. I must stay closer to him than I had wanted to. I can't afford to lose him now.

Zack drives fast. I am having difficulty keeping up with him, yet staying far enough back so that he won't see me. I don't pay much attention to where we are going until he pulls up at a small apartment house on a quiet street, turns off the lights, slams the door of his car, and runs up the steps to vanish inside.

What do I do now? Do I follow him? Maybe I had better just wait here until he leaves, then go inside the apartment house and find out whom he might be seeing.

This apartment house surprises me. I can't

imagine who lives in it whom Zack would hurry to see.

I roll down the window to get some fresh air. The night is humid and full of the smell of stale grass cuttings. A mound of large black garbage bags lies next to the curb, waiting for the morning's pickup, I suppose. Old, tired trees have cracked the sidewalk with their roots, and someone's overloud television set shouts from across the lawn.

It would be a good idea to walk to the corner, read the name of this street, and jot it down along with the address of the apartment house, I think. I am reaching for the door handle when suddenly, through the open window, an arm shoots in, and a strong hand covers my mouth!

TWELVE

"**D**ON'T MAKE a sound! What are you doing here?"

I gasp as the hand withdraws and I stare into the face of the man leaning in my car window. It's Kelly!

"You scared me to death!" I tell him.

"Sorry," Kelly says. "What are you doing?"

"I called Zack. When I talked to him, I whispered, so he couldn't tell who I was. I just told him to meet me. He drove here, and I followed him."

Kelly thinks a moment, then nods his head. "Not a bad idea. So this must be the place."

I shiver. "Kelly, the third person must live

in those apartments. Should we call Detective York?"

"No!" Kelly says quickly. "We have no proof. We don't even know which of the apartments Zack is in. You just told him to meet you. What if he thought you were his bookie?"

"Come on, Kelly," I mutter. An idea hits me. "Just what are you doing here, by the way?"

"I was driving over to talk to Zack," Kelly says. "I'd just reached the cross street near his house when I saw him turn the corner and saw your car behind his. So I came along for the ride."

"Why were you going to talk to him?"

"You tried talking to Loretta, and that didn't work. I thought maybe I could approach Zack through his ego, maybe lead him into giving something away."

"So here we are. Should we see who lives in that apartment house?"

"I think we ought to get out of here before Zack comes out. He's probably made his contact and is steamed about being out on a wildgoose chase. He should be storming out of there in a couple of minutes."

"If we wait, we might see who's with him."

"Go home, Christina," Kelly savs "You're taking too big a chance being here."

"Just what are you planning to do?"

"I'll tail him to his house. When he gets home, I'll talk to him. Now go home."

"Wait a minute! This was my idea! And I've got to check the apartment mailboxes and find out who lives there."

"I can take care of that."

"When?"

"After I talk to Zack."

"But..."

"Trust me," Kelly says. "I'll get the information for you. Now be a good girl and go home. I'll be over tomorrow."

"What time?"

"Tomorrow's Saturday, and I don't go to work until two. How about if I come around eleven?"

"All right." I turn on the ignition. That uncomfortable thought is skittering around in my brain again. If it would just hold still for a second, I might be able to capture it. I wave good-bye to Kelly and drive down the street, turning the corner.

I'm about three blocks away when I begin to wonder if Kelly will be safe. What if Zack comes out with that third person? What if they see Kelly and want to get rid of him? He might need help. I don't want to leave him in a tight situation. I'd better go back.

I go around another couple of corners and back to that street, whose name is now implanted in my memory. I don't park in the same place. Zack's car is still there, but Kelly's car is gone. What happened to Kelly? I thought he was tailing Zack.

I cut my lights and pull up under a sagging mimosa tree. I'm fairly well hidden here, and with the help of the nearby streetlight I can see anyone who might come in or out of the apartment house. I wonder why Zack hasn't left the building yet.

Suddenly the door opens, and Zack appears. Without looking to the left or right, he hurries to his car, gets in, and takes off.

Where is Kelly? I wish one of us had been able to see what apartment Zack had been in. What's Kelly up to? I'm so impatient I can't stand it.

The street is silent. It's dark. I feel very much alone. But there's no one to stop me now. I've got to do what I had in mind. I'm going into the apartment house to read the names on the mailboxes. Kelly said he'd take care of that, but I think I'd better do it just to make sure. One of those names should give me a clue. I cautiously climb from my car, shutting the door as softly as I can. I'm afraid of the darkness of the street, of the silence, but mostly I'm afraid of what I might find in that apartment house. I'm terrified that I'm going to recognize one of those names!

Up the steps and through the unlocked door I go, into a cramped lobby. There is a dusty plastic plant in a clay pot on a rickety table, and a light rectangle in the paint above it where a picture had once hung. On the opposite side are the rows of little mailbox doors—sixteen of them, each with a first initial and last name printed on cards on the doors. I scan the names quickly, but none is familiar. So I pull a pencil out of my handbag and fish around for something to write on. The back of an envelope will have to do. I copy each name as fast as

I can, occasionally darting swift glances over my shoulder to make sure no one has come into the lobby and is watching me.

C. Washington, F. Ferris, A. Gonzalez, K. Smith...I scribble the names on the envelope. The small room reeks of stale, rancid odors left by many tenants over many years. I'm eager to leave.

There is the sound of a door closing upstairs, and I hear footsteps over my head. I rush through the front door into the darkness, run as fast as I can to my car, and lock myself in. I wait, motionless, until the door to the apartment house opens and a couple strolls out. They walk down the street aimlessly, away from me. Where they are going I don't care. I'm able to breathe again, so I start the car and drive home.

I go over the names in my mind while I'm driving, and after I'm in bed, wanting to fall asleep. An idea begins to slip around where I can't touch it. I grab at it again and again, but it teases and taunts, then slithers away. Exhausted, I roll on my side, knees tucked up, arms pressed against my chest, abandoning the chase, drifting into sleep.

And it comes.

The idea, miffed at being abandoned in midchase, flings itself into my conscious mind. I am so startled that my eyes fly open and I gasp. Of course! It's the answer! It bothered me at the time it was said, but it didn't completely register. Only the person working with those people would have known about that—only that person and me. Because I know. And I must tell someone!

I phone Kelly. A sleepy voice answers, grumping around the words. "Do you know what time it is?" Kelly's mother asks.

But another voice breaks in on an extension—Kelly's. "It's all right, Mom," he says. "I've got it."

She listens for a moment, then apparently decides she is too sleepy to be curious, and I hear the receiver click in its cradle.

"Christina? What's on your mind?" Kelly asks.

"What happened after I left the apartment building?"

"Is that all you called for?" He sounds disappointed.

"Please tell me, Kelly."

"There's not much to tell. I followed Zack home, and talked to him for a while, to see if he'd give out any information."

"Did he?"

"Nothing new."

"How about the names?"

"What names?"

"The names of the people who live in that apartment house."

"Oh, sure. I've got them written down somewhere. None of them meant anything to me. I'll give you the list."

"How did you know I'd talked to Loretta?" I ask.

There is a pause, and Kelly gives an abrupt laugh. "Don't you remember, Christina? You told me you talked to her."

I want to say, "Oh, Kelly, I trusted you. I wanted you as a friend. Why did you lie to me?" But instead I say, "Kelly, I couldn't sleep. I needed to talk to you."

"Well, relax," Kelly says. "Try to get some sleep. I'll be over tomorrow at eleven. Is that still okay?"

"It's okay," I answer, and I slowly hang up.

I have to make one more call. I scoot out of

bed, find the card with Detective York's phone numbers on it, and climb back in bed, sitting cross-legged, the phone on my lap.

He's not on duty, so I call his home number. It's not too late, I hope.

He answers on the first ring, and I'm glad to know I didn't wake him up. I hear music in the background and some people laughing.

"This is Christina," I tell him. "I know who the third person is."

His answer is deliberate. "How do you know?"

"Something that was said a few days ago. I just realized how it fit in."

"Do you have any proof that would stand up in court?"

"No," I say, "but it's something to work on."

He sighs. "Christina, it may be a long, drawn-out process, if that's all you've got."

"There's something else," I tell him. "Some names on mailboxes in an apartment house. I'm guessing, but I think one of them will tie in to the kidnapping."

"Listen," he says, "stop doing things on your own. We'll get together and compare notes. I've got some sheets from the records department. Putting them together with what you've got may help."

"Can you come by tomorrow morning—around eleven?" I ask.

"You wouldn't rather come downtown?"

"I think it's important," I say. "I think some-one will be here who…" I interrupt myself, pleading. "Please be here! Please!"

"Eleven o'clock? I guess I can work that in, if nothing urgent comes up."

"Thank you."

"Good night, Christina," he says, and I hear a click and a dead sound. I put the re-ceiver in its cradle and place the phone on the floor.

I sit in the middle of my bed, my arms wrapped around my legs, my chin resting on my knees. I have to think.

For some reason I'm not as unhappy or disturbed as I thought I would be. There is a certain elation at discovering this third per-son, a certain disappointment in the people I trusted, and a growing self-confidence in my-self as a person. It's all mixed up, but my feel-ings are more up than they are down.

I can't even remember the Christina who

was, before the kidnapping took place, years and years and years ago. That Christina was fumbling around, following orders, doing all the right things, and wishing she knew who and what she was all about. She was a child who thought the most important thing in her life was going to be a trip to France her parents didn't want her to take.

But the Christina I feel inside me now reminds me of those potted spring bulbs with tiny shoots strong enough to break through the pebbles packed over them, strong enough to reach up to the light and grow and grow and bloom and fulfill themselves. I am the shoot... not up very far...and I know I've got a long way to grow. But it's good knowing I've come this far. I've got a direction now. It will take a lot more thought, a lot more discovery, but I know where I'm going. That's what counts.

I roll over and go to sleep on my stomach, arms and legs flung wide. Tomorrow will come soon, and there will be some risk involved in what I plan to do. But I'm not afraid.

Surprisingly, I sleep until nearly ten. I dash into a pair of jeans and a yellow T-shirt and hurry into the kitchen to bolt down a quick breakfast. The front of my shirt has a massive lion's head covering it. Very appropriate.

"Why the rush?" my mother asks. She pours herself another cup of coffee and sits beside me. Della putters in and out from the kitchen to the laundry room and back.

"I've got somewhere to go," I sputter, filling my mouth with cornflakes and trying to talk around them.

"But where, darling?" She puts down her cup with a tiny click against the saucer. "Christina, wouldn't it be lovely if we could take a day together to shop and lunch and... well, sort things out? We could talk."

"About what?" The orange juice goes down in one long gulp.

My mother sighs and lightly rests a hand on my arm. "Madame DeJon phoned me, Christina. She was concerned about your absence."

"I was here," I tell her. "You tucked me in bed and brought me chicken soup. Remember?"

"She was afraid the illness was somewhat psychosomatic. She was afraid you had been unhappy with the attitude of some of the students when you returned to school after..." My mother is unable to complete the sentence.

"She may be right," I say, putting down my spoon and facing her for the first time that morning. "It was a rotten day. It was really the pits. I didn't want to see those people again."

"But school..."

"Don't worry, Mother." I smile and hug her. "I've taken care of that problem. I'll be at school on Monday."

Relief smooths the tired lines from her face. "I'm so glad, Christina. I know it's difficult, but..."

I haven't time for a replay, so I jump up give her a quick kiss on her forehead, and say, "But I've got to leave now, Mother. I'll take a rain check on the lunch and shopping."

I hurry out the front door, avoiding the busy laundry room, and circle around to the garage.

It doesn't take long to drive to the Tigus house. As I hoped, Zack's car is gone. Now, if only Loretta is there! She has to be! I pull my car up on the driveway, close to the back door, and hop out.

She doesn't answer at first, as I pound on the back door, but I can hear her inside, feel her listening intently on the other side of the wooden door.

"Loretta Tigus!" I yell. "Open this door, or I'll get a hatchet and break it down!"

It opens immediately and she stares at me. A little bubble of saliva begins to drip from her open mouth, and she nervously rubs a hand across her lips.

"What do you think you're doing?" she asks.

I take her arm, gripping her tightly around one wrist, and tug her through the doorway. "I'm going to take you to meet someone," I tell her.

She tries to pull away, but my determination has given me strength she'll never have. She grabs at the door frame and hangs on with all her might.

"Loretta," I tell her, grunting and pulling, "I'm going to raise hell out here if you don't come with me! There isn't a neighbor for blocks around who won't come running. And someone will call the police!"

"But...I gotta ask Zack."

"You don't have to ask him anything anymore. I say that you're coming with me! Now, come!"

Maybe it's my tone of voice. Maybe Loretta is just used to obeying orders. Suddenly she lets go of the door frame, nearly goes limp, and it's all I can do to keep my balance. We practically tumble down the rickety steps.

I lead her to the car and make her slide in from the driver's side. She immediately tries the handle on the passenger side, but it's locked.

"Forget it," I tell her. "It's one of those safety locks that can be opened only by the driver."

I back out of the driveway and head home. A quick glance at my watch shows me that the timing is right. I hope Detective York is there when I arrive. And I hope Kelly is there, too.

I turn to glance at Loretta. She is sitting upright, her hands gripped together. Strings of hair hang around her face, loose from the rubber band she had used to tie it back. Her eyes are dull, and she stares straight ahead.

"When did you last see Kelly?" I ask her.

She looks at me, startled. She reminds me

of a little sparrow that has come to snatch a bread crumb, but flutters around it nervously, ready to fly away at the sign of a cat.

"I don't know," she says.

"You answered my other question," I tell her.

"What other question are you talking about? You only asked me one."

"Loretta," I say, easing around a repair crew that blocks half the street, "you'll have to tell the truth about what happened."

"I told my story," she says. Her lips press together in a tight line.

"Zack told your story. You just repeated everything he told you to say."

She doesn't answer.

"Loretta, we know who the third person is. We know who worked the kidnapping out and who planned all those things so that if you didn't get away it would look as though I had set up a con to steal money from my grandmother."

"You can't know." Her voice is just a whisper. "Zack said no one could find out."

"Zack isn't that bright."

"And you think you know everything?" Her voice is a sneer.

"No, but I do know the name of everyone involved, and I know that you're going to tell the truth about what happened," I tell her.

"And get killed for it?"

Loretta is really scared now, and I reassure her. "You aren't going to get killed. What makes you think you'll get killed?"

"You said I might."

"I was guessing."

"Zack said so, too, when I told him what you said. He said I'd be likely to get killed if I talked about it to anybody."

"Was it you who phoned me? Or Zack? Or…" But I've lost her. Loretta is off in thoughts of her own—frightening thoughts, I can tell by the expression on her face.

We're close to home, and I'm nervous myself. What if it doesn't work? Then we go into the long, drawn-out investigating, maybe letting this third person escape. My plan has to work!

Loretta doesn't seem to be aware of our surroundings until I slow down and pull into the drive in front of our house. There are two other cars parked there—Kelly's little orange Volkswagen, and another car, which I hope belongs to Detective York. I've forgotten what he looks like.

"What are we doing here?" Loretta screeches. "You can't take me here!"

"You have to face it now, Loretta." I hit the brakes, and we stop suddenly. She frantically grapples with the door handle and I'm not sure I can hold her, so I lay on the horn.

In a moment the front door opens. Detective York and Kelly run outside, my mother right behind them. Detective York lopes to Loretta's side of the car. I release the door lock, so when she throws the door open she practically falls into his arms.

Loretta looks around wildly, the whites of her eyes rimming the pupils. In a way I feel sorry for her.

"Where's Della?" I ask my mother.

She looks almost as frightened as Loretta. "Why...in the kitchen, I guess. I don't know... Somewhere in the house."

"Bring Loretta inside," I shout, and run

into the house. Behind me I can hear Loretta screaming, "No! No!"

It takes a few minutes to find Della. She is huddled behind the front stairway, trying unsuccessfully to compress her large body into something small and invisible. Her face contorts as she sees me. She looks as though she is going to burst into tears.

The others come up behind me, and as she faces all of us, Della straightens. "What's this woman doing here?" she asks. She avoids looking directly at Loretta.

"She came to identify you," I tell Della.

"No!" Loretta shrieks again. "I didn't say nothing! I told Zack I wouldn't say nothing!"

Della lets out a long sigh that ripples through her heavy body like ocean swells in a calm sea. "I didn't think you'd push so hard to find out," she says. "I thought everybody would just forget about it sooner or later, since Christina didn't get hurt."

Kelly is incredulous. "Della is the third person?"

"Not exactly," I tell him. I turn to Detective York. "I've got that list of last names and first initials from the mailboxes in the apartment house I told you about. The address is on the paper. I think you'll find the name of Della's son on that list. He'd have a different last name from hers, so I couldn't recognize it. If my guess is right, he's the one who worked out the idea. You'll probably also find out that he met Zack when they were in jail together."

"How did you find this out?" Kelly asks.

"From something Della said," I tell him. "I didn't recognize it at the time, but it kept nagging at me. Della said something about 'that woman's rent house.' I read all the newspaper stories and couldn't find anything about their house. I realized that information wouldn't have been on the television news either. The only way Della could know this would be if she knew Zack and Loretta. That was my only clue. Then when I went into the apartment house and wrote down the names, I realized there had to be another person, too—and that person was probably Della's son. He thought of the plan and got Della and Zack to go along with it."

"One more thing added up," I say. "I remembered a man in Zack's hamburger place who didn't stare at me when Zack came to my table with Loretta and made the commotion. And I realized that he didn't look my way because he knew what Zack was setting up. He was in on it. I'm sure he is Della's son."

It doesn't take long for Detective York to call in for a blue-and-white patrol car to take Della and Loretta in; and he makes arrangements for Della's son and Zack to be picked up. My mother flutters over me for a while, then goes to the den to phone my grandmother. My father is speaking at a youth group luncheon. She'll have to fill him in later.

I'm left with Kelly to talk to, and I make it short. "You ought to get an 'A' on this project," I say. "Or are you after bigger game, like a full scholarship to pay your tuition so you won't have to work while you're going to school?"

He opens his mouth to protest, thinks better of it, and says quietly, "Both, I hope."

"I hadn't told you I talked to Loretta. You found that out from Loretta. And you found out enough from Loretta or Zack to lead you to that apartment house. I bet that last night you were checking out names on the apartment mailboxes when Zack came charging through the front door, and you ran out the back, circling around and scaring me to death."

"I followed Zack a number of times," he admits. "Once he led me to that apartment house. I thought there might be someone living there who tied in with the kidnapping."

"You were pumping Zack and Loretta for information, and you were pumping me, too. You wanted to break this case yourself."

"Listen, Christina," Kelly says, "I did try to help you."

"Yes, you did, and I'm glad you did. I might not have been able to do it alone. I just wish you hadn't used me. I wish you hadn't lied to me."

"Would you have talked to me and worked with me if I'd told you I was interested in solving the case just to get a scholarship in communications?"

"No."

Kelly spreads out his hands in an open gesture and tries to grin. "There...you see."

"I see one thing, Kelly—that you're an opportunist. There was a time when you could have left me shattered, but not now. I can look at you without feeling betrayed."

"Betrayed? Come on, isn't that a pretty strong word?" he asks me.

"Who cares? I don't."

I walk toward the door. Kelly follows. "Christina, I think I can get a pretty good job with the TV channel I'm working for—you know, looking ahead to after graduation—if you don't call in the press for a little while. You understand? I'd like an exclusive."

I take a long look at him. "I'm not going to call anyone in yet, Kelly. You can do what you like."

"I mean, you were eager to have people know the truth about you."

"They will."

There's a long pause. Kelly looks uncomfortable. Finally he says, "Well, thanks, Christina. Aren't you going to wish me luck?"

"You don't need it," I say. "I expect you to be very successful and get everything you want out of life. It's the people who deal with you who'll need the luck."

I stand aside, and Kelly leaves. I watch his

little orange car chug down the driveway; then I shut the door.

My mother comes in and wraps her arms around me. There are tears in her eyes. "It's all over now, darling," she says.

I hug her in return and answer, "Not completely, Mother. I think I've got my head on straight now, so there's one more thing to do."

She backs off, holding my shoulders, looking at me with a puzzled expression.

"As I told you, I'm going back to school Monday," I say. "But also, Monday I'm going hunting for a part-time job. I don't want Cristabel's trust fund with all those strings attached. If it were a gift, let's face it, I'd enjoy using the money for my education. But it's not a gift, and I don't need it. Lots of people work their way through college. I can, too. I'm going to tell Cristabel that I've found out that I'm really very much like her in some ways. I'm just as stubborn and determined as she is."

"But Cristabel has your schooling all planned! She won't like this!" My mother is gripping her hands together as though trying to hold something that is slipping away.

"Listen to me, Mother," I say. "I don't need Cristabel's ideas or her money. I can make it on my own. And it's going to mean more to me when I do."

"But Cristabel can give you so much!"

"Not as much as I can give myself."

I run upstairs, smiling a little, humming a tune off-key. I feel good about myself. I've got to tell Lorna someday that I've found out what is really important—I am. It's a great feeling.

Have you read these
Joan Lowery Nixon books?

The Séance

WINNER OF THE EDGAR ALLAN POE AWARD
FOR BEST YOUNG ADULT MYSTERY

The séance starts as a game, but it leads to
murder and terror for a small Texas town.

A Deadly Game of Magic

Lisa and her friends find themselves
in a cat-and-mouse game with
a murderous magician.